mary-kateandashley

Sweet 16

Look for these

Sweet 16

titles:

1 Never Been Kissed
2 Wishes and Dreams
3 The Perfect Summer
4 Getting There
5 Starring You and Me
6 My Best Friend's Boyfriend
7 Playing Games
8 Cross Our Hearts
9 All That Glitters
10 Keeping Secrets
11 Little White Lies
12 Dream Holiday
13 Love and Kisses

mary-kateandashley

Sweet 16

SPRING INTO STYLE

Laurel Stowe Brady

HarperCollins*Entertainment*
An Imprint of HarperCollins*Publishers*

A PARACHUTE PRESS BOOK

A PARACHUTE PRESS BOOK
Parachute Publishing, LLC
156 Fifth Avenue
Suite 325
NEW YORK
NY 10010

First published in the USA by HarperEntertainment 2002
First published in Great Britain by HarperCollins*Entertainment* 2006
HarperCollins*Entertainment* is an imprint of HarperCollins*Publishers* Ltd,
77-85 Fulham Palace Road, Hammersmith, London W6 8JB

SWEET 16 books are created and produced by Parachute Press, LLC, in cooperation with Dualstar Publications, a division of Dualstar Entertainment Group, LLC, published by HarperEntertainment, an imprint of HarperCollins Publishers.

The HarperCollins website address is
www.fireandwater.com

1 3 5 7 9 8 6 4 2

ISBN-13 978 0 00 718108 7
ISBN-10 0 00 718108 6

Printed and bound in Great Britain by Clays Ltd, St Ives plc

chapter one

"Just think, eight glorious days with no school!" I said.

"I'm going to sleep late every single day." My friend Brittany Bowen sighed in happy anticipation of freedom.

"Not me!" my sister, Mary-Kate, said. "Think of all that extra time for activities!"

Our friends Lauren Glazer, Brittany Bowen, and Melanie Han were celebrating the start of spring break with Mary-Kate and me by wandering through the mall after school. It was a gorgeous Friday afternoon, and none of us wanted to go home yet.

"Oh, Ashley," Lauren said as we passed Sparkle Palace, an accessories store. "I need to stop in here. I broke my hair clip just before gym today."

"I noticed," I said with a grin. "But I like how you improvised."

Lauren smiled and touched her loosely gathered ponytails, which were held in place with twist ties. "You like them, Ashley? They're all the rage. Luckily, my gym teacher had lots of these on hand for her storage bags." Her blue eyes twinkled.

"Lucky for you she wasn't using those plastic bags with zip tops," Mary-Kate joked.

"I'll catch up with you guys later," Lauren called as she dashed into the store.

Brittany tugged Mary-Kate's arm. "Mmmmm, I recognize that smell!" She and Mary-Kate grinned at each other. "The Nuthouse," they chimed together.

Brittany slipped her arm through Mary-Kate's. "Come on, let's get some roasted nuts." Brittany was one of those lucky girls who could eat anything and still keep her model-thin figure.

"Good idea," Mary-Kate said. "I smell a bag of nuts with my name on it."

Melanie shook her head, tossing her straight dark hair from shoulder to shoulder. "Not for me. We're having dinner early tonight."

"None for me either," I said. "I'm kind of full after the trail mix I had at lunch." I nodded toward one of my favorite stores, Glitter and Glam. "You guys get nuts while Melanie and I check out what's new."

"All right," Brittany said. "We'll tell Lauren where we're going."

Mary-Kate checked her watch. "Then I'll have to book over to *Girlz*."

Girlz is a hot fashion magazine aimed at teens. Mary-Kate has a great part-time job at their offices.

Brittany and Mary-Kate headed off one way while Melanie and I went the other. We hurried over to the brightly lit storefront of Glitter and Glam.

Inside, Melanie tugged me over to the makeup counter. "Try that glittery bronze eye shadow," she suggested. "It'll bring out the blue in your eyes."

Melanie always knows what will look good. She's the most fashionable of our friends. And no wonder—her father is in the fashion business. He's always bringing back the coolest clothes from Paris, Milan, and Tokyo for Melanie.

I picked up the tester and applied a bit to my left eyelid. Melanie was right; it was a great color for me.

A dark-haired woman in a stylish orange-plaid suit hurried over to us. She looked straight out of a top fashion magazine.

"Hello, girls," the woman greeted us. "My name is Jennifer Lewis. I'm the owner of Glitter and Glam."

"Oh, we love your store, Ms. Lewis!" Melanie exclaimed.

"It's our favorite," I added.

Ms. Lewis smiled. "Glad to hear that!"

I noticed she wore a big button pinned to her jacket with the words "Teen Trends" on it.

"What's the button for?" I asked.

"That's exactly what I wanted to talk to you two girls about," Ms. Lewis said. "A number of the mall store owners are sponsoring a spring break Teen Trend-Spotter Contest. We're looking for just the right teens to become contestants. Would you two like to be in it?"

"A trend-spotting contest? What's that?" I asked.

"Trend-spotters are people who keep their eyes open for anything and everything that might influence fashion," Ms. Lewis explained. "Things like music, celebrities, movies, sports—even clothes you see other kids wearing. Whatever might turn into the next hot fashion trend."

"People get paid for that kind of thing?" Melanie asked.

"Kids our age?" I added.

Ms. Lewis nodded. "Yes. In fact, there are teens all over the country who have part-time jobs spotting trends."

"What a great job!" I said.

"You girls wouldn't be paid for this," Ms. Lewis explained, "but the winner of the contest will get a shopping spree at her favorite store."

A shopping spree? I couldn't think of a better prize!

"That's payment enough for me!" I told her. "Where do I sign up?"

"It's going to be hard work," Ms. Lewis cautioned. "You should consider participating only if you are serious about it. But you look like young ladies who would enjoy a challenge." She smiled and stepped back a bit, as if to give us room to think.

"It sounds perfect for you, Ashley," Melanie said, "but I don't think I'd be very good at it."

"Of course you would," I said. "You have a real eye for what looks just right."

"Well, I don't know. . . ."

"Come on, Melanie," I said, not wanting her to miss this chance. "This is something you were born to do!" I smiled at Ms. Lewis. "What do we need to do?" I asked her.

Ms. Lewis handed us applications and a meeting schedule. "Just fill in this form." Her brown eyes twinkled. "I knew you'd both be terrific trend-spotters the minute I saw you. I mean, that vest, for instance," she said, pointing to Melanie. "Vests like that are the hottest thing in Europe right now. But we don't expect them to hit here until next spring. It's very cutting-edge."

"Oh, um, thanks," Melanie said.

I was surprised. Melanie *loves* talking about clothes. But she didn't sound very excited.

Suddenly Melanie handed the papers back to Ms. Lewis. "I'm really sorry, but I just remembered I . . . um . . . have a job this spring break. I won't be able to do this." She turned to me. "Ashley? I need to pick something up at the drugstore. I'll see you there." She turned and hurried out of the store.

I stared after her. A job? I happened to know that she *didn't* have a job this spring break. *What was up with Melanie?*

chapter two

I spotted Melanie hurrying past the pretzel stand on her way to the mall exit. "Wait, Melanie!" I called.

"I don't want to talk about it, Ashley," she yelled back at me, then quickened her pace.

I ran after her and caught her arm. "Who are you and what have you done with the real Melanie? The real Melanie would jump at a chance like this!"

She shook off my hand. "Please leave me alone, Ashley."

I crossed my arms over my chest and looked her straight in the eye. "You don't have a job next week. I know it and you know it. So why did you say that you did?"

"I just don't want to be a stupid trend-spotter."

My heart sank. The contest wouldn't be as much fun without Melanie. "How many times are you going to walk into the mall and get picked out of the crowd to do something fun like this!" I said. "Doesn't that count for something?"

She didn't answer. She just started walking again, almost stomping as if she was angry.

I followed her and gave it one more shot. "I don't get it. This is perfect for someone like you. You're so smart about what's hot, what's cool, what's fashionable."

Melanie stopped walking and spun around to face me. "Who says I'm smart about clothes and fashion? I'll tell you what I am, and that is *sick* of fashion. It's all I hear about at home, all my dad ever talks about. So once and for all, I am totally not interested in this contest. Or anything else connected with fashion."

"But that's not true," I insisted. "You love everything about fashion. You always have." This was so confusing—Melanie practically breathed fashion night and day. "Everyone always says you're going to wind up being a designer or a magazine editor someday."

Melanie let out a frustrated grunt. "Why does everyone assume I want a fashion career anyway?"

"All right, explain to me how you can *not* want to have a fashion career. You're genetically programmed to be all about fashion. I mean, look at your dad!"

Melanie glared at me and put her hands on her hips. "Exactly!" She was really mad now. "Okay, fine, I'll admit it. I've always had a thing for fashion. But my dad is so brilliant and so well known all over the world. He's considered some kind of genius. If I tried to do anything fashion oriented, everybody would just think I'm trying to cash in on his name. The worst part is, maybe they'd be right. Maybe I don't have any real fashion sense of my own."

"Oh, Melanie. Are you kidding? You heard what the lady said about your vest!"

"That's exactly what I mean." Melanie grabbed the lapel of her vest and shook it at me. "Who do you think picked this out? My dad, that's who. So, you see, that lady who was so impressed with my trend-spotting skills was not seeing my skills at all. She was seeing my *dad's*."

"Your dad may have picked out that vest, but that doesn't mean *you* wouldn't have if you'd been there," I said.

Melanie took a deep breath. "All right. What if I do go along with this thing and I completely blow it? How stupid would I feel? Worse than that, what would my dad say? I don't want to embarrass him and I don't want to humiliate myself."

"Correct me if I'm wrong," I said slowly, "but I think the bottom line here is that you're a total chicken."

Melanie's brown eyes widened. "Don't you dare call me a chicken," she snapped at me. "I'm not a chicken. I'm just"—she searched for the right word—"a realist."

I shook my head. "No, you're a chicken. The truth is, you're afraid you won't live up to your dad's expectations. And that's just plain silly. And unfair."

"How is it silly and unfair?" Melanie scowled.

"It's silly of you and unfair to your dad. That would be like me saying, 'Oh no! I can't sing in the school play. My dad's in the music business. If I stink he might not love me anymore.' "

Melanie stared at me for a second, but then she burst out laughing. I laughed, too. It was such a silly thing to say, but I guess it was exactly what Melanie needed to hear to snap her out of it.

"Come on," I said, "the contest will be much more fun if we both do it. Besides, what have you got to lose?"

Melanie smiled. "On the top-ten list of famous last words, 'What have you got to lose?' ranks number one."

"No way," I said. How could this possibly turn out wrong?

❀

"Make way, Mary-Kate," Liam called out. He struggled through the door of the little cubicle that served as our office at *Girlz* magazine with a heavy box. "Coming through."

"Gotta go, Ashley," I said into my cell phone and clicked off. She'd just called and told me all about the trend-spotters contest. She sounded really excited.

I stared at the huge box Liam plopped in the center of the floor. "More?" I groaned. It was the third box already.

"This is the last one for now." Liam smiled. "Come on, Mary-Kate, this is fun. Just like opening Christmas presents."

"Not exactly." I sighed. "You would think we'd have more exciting things to do than make lists of product samples."

"Somebody's gotta do it, and it might as well be you and me," Liam said, slicing through the heavy tape sealing the package. "After all, we can't expect all the best assignments. I mean, we're still pretty new around here."

"I thought I was the one who lucked out this spring break with this great job," I said. "But Ashley's got me beat with her trend-spotting gig."

I quickly told Liam about what happened to Ashley and Melanie after I left the mall.

"That does sound like something she'd be good at," Liam said. "But come on, Mary-Kate. Think about it. How many high school kids get to have a part-time job working for a cool magazine and actually see their names in print like we did?"

"That's true," I said. We'd worked at *Girlz* only for a short time, and already we'd both written articles that were printed in the magazine.

"With any luck, we'll get to write some more articles soon," I said. I knelt down beside the large carton. "And it *is* kind of fun to be the first to see the latest, newest makeup samples before anybody else does."

"That's the spirit," Liam said.

I pulled out one of several small packages from inside the box, ripped it open, then turned it upside down and shook out the contents.

Toothbrushes. I waved one at Liam. "How thrilling."

"Just think," Liam said. "Once we get this all unpacked and inventoried, we can get to the fun part—figuring out what we can write about all this stuff so that it sounds mind-blowingly awesome."

"The can't-live-without-it angle," I said. I stared at the toothbrush. "Speak to me," I joked. I shook my head. "*Nada.* Zip. Nothing." I tossed the toothbrush back into the box.

"Inspiration will hit," Liam said. "It always does."

Suddenly our boss, C.K., appeared out of nowhere, snapping her fingers from the doorway to get our attention.

C.K. knows only one speed and it's full throttle—she goes fast, thinks fast, talks fast. Everybody around her has to do the same or they get mowed down.

She pointed at us. "Both of you. Ten minutes. My office."

I felt my face go red. I hoped she didn't think we were just goofing off in here.

"I'm off to Europe," C.K. said. "The car will be here in"—she glanced at her watch—"twelve minutes. So you'll have exactly two minutes to run your ideas for the July issue past me before I'm out of here. Amaze me."

Then she was gone, back to her office.

Oh. My. Gosh.

I turned to Liam, panic stricken. "Ten minutes! What are we going to do?"

"We're going to think like crazy, Mary-Kate," he said. "So think, quick! We need ideas, ideas, ideas. Now!"

I stared at him. He sounded exactly like C.K. That only made my brain freeze up. "My mind is a total blank," I wailed. "We are so dead."

"Don't think that way," he ordered. "Stay positive."

I looked wildly around the room. "Okay, let's brainstorm. Quick, what do we have here?"

I pawed through a nearby pile of lip gloss, makeup sponges, and eyeliners. Nothing came to me. I grabbed a sleek bottle of astringent.

"Pores . . . pores . . . pour . . . something about pouring. . . . Pour over . . . poor little pores? Oh, that's awful." I tossed it aside and grabbed a small bottle of foundation. "The foundation of summer skin care . . ." I set the bottle on the desk and looked over at Liam. "Come on, Liam, a little help here?"

"How about the old standard?" He held up a razor. "Something about a close shave? Nah, that's been done to death."

"July," I said. "Sunburn month? Vacations . . . Just because you're on vacation, don't forget to take care of your . . . ?"

Aaargh! The clock was ticking and we were getting nowhere fast.

Liam pulled a glittery toothbrush from the package I'd opened. "How about toothbrushes—the hottest new shapes for the hottest kids. . . ."

I raised an eyebrow at him.

He tossed the toothbrush back into the box. "You're right," he said. "That's terrible." He glanced around the room. "How about . . . How about . . ."

"How about how not to pull your hair completely out when you're stressed." I moaned, yanking my hair. "Why did I ever think working at a magazine would be a cool job?"

"Wait. Stop!" Liam snapped his fingers. *"Cool job!* That's good. That's the story. Something like 'Cool jobs for hot kids.' "

I froze in mid hair pull. "Hmmm. You've got my attention." I perched on the edge of the messy desk. "Keep going."

Liam pointed a pen at me. "How about this: you could follow Ashley around for a day and write an article about her trend-spotting. No! Wait!" He jumped up and walked around the room. "Even better. We can do a whole article on summer jobs. We could each spend a day watching—no, wait—" He held up both his hands as if he were stopping traffic. "This is even better! We'll each spend a day actually *doing* different jobs, and then write about the good, the bad, and the ugly of each."

"Way to think fast, Liam." I was impressed. "C.K. will love it."

"Thank you." He took a bow, and then grabbed a notepad and a pen. "All we need to do now is think of some jobs we could focus on." He tapped the pen on the pad and bit his lip.

"That's easy. Lifeguarding could be one," I volunteered.

"And coffee-bar waiter," Liam suggested.

"Dog walker," I said.

Liam nodded, writing down all of our ideas. "This could be good."

"It's better than good," I said. "It's going to be a blast." I gave him a high five.

The intercom on the desk buzzed. "Meeting," a voice crackled. "C.K.'s office. Now."

"Good luck to us," I whispered as I followed Liam down the hall.

C.K. sat at her desk, yanking files from a drawer and tossing them into an open leather case. "Fire away, and you'd better impress me," she said, slamming the drawer shut with her foot as she scooted herself in the wheeled chair backward to a file cabinet.

Liam nudged me. "Go ahead," he whispered.

"No, you, it's your idea," I hissed.

"He who hesitates is lost," C.K. barked, scooting back to her desk to buzz someone else.

Liam kicked me.

"Okay." I took a deep breath. "We were thinking—"

C.K.'s travel manager, Phil, rushed in.

"Yes, C.K.?" he asked.

"Tickets," C.K. barked.

Phil scurried out.

"You were thinking . . ." C.K. slapped the leather case shut.

I gulped, then blurted out, "We want to do an article called 'Hot kids, cool jobs,' about kids who—"

"I love it." C.K. stood up as Phil rushed in to hand her a small packet.

"And sign these," he said, thrusting a stack of papers at C.K.

"We thought we'd each work at different jobs for a day," I continued.

"Sign these? What are these? Glasses." C.K. stuck out her hand as she squinted at the papers.

"Uh . . . they're on your head," Liam said.

"So they are." C.K. yanked her glasses onto her nose, not even looking at us. "You know what, Mary-Kate? It's great. I don't need all the picky details, it's going to be good. You'll help her out, right, Liam? You've got a real future in this business, Mary-Kate."

"But it wasn't my—" I began.

The desk phone rang. Phil picked it up. "Car's here," he announced.

"Okay, I'm gone. Liam," C.K. said as she gathered up her papers, briefcase, purse, and jacket, "I can't spare you both away from the office while I'm gone, so I want Mary-Kate to take this thing and run with it. She'll go out and do the jobs while you stay in the office. Keep things on track and edit what Mary-Kate turns in after each of her gigs."

"But it was Liam's—" I tried again.

C.K. ignored me and hurried down the hallway toward the elevator. Liam and I followed behind her as several people popped out of their offices and tried to get her attention. One of C.K.'s assistants stuck some papers in her hand and hurried to explain them. The elevator stopped, and we all tumbled in. C.K.'s personal assistant, Terri, scribbled in a notebook while C.K. went on giving orders.

"Make sure to fax those page dummies as soon as they're ready. And get that photo shoot scheduled before our top choice gets booked up."

"C.K.," I tried again. "It was Liam's—"

The elevator door popped open and we all scurried out. "Not now, Mary-Kate," C.K. said. "Terri, get me a couple of copies of whatever Janet scheduled and fax them to me."

We stood on the curb as someone yanked the car door open and C.K. slipped in. The car door slammed, and then she was gone. Everyone drifted back inside and upstairs.

Liam and I were left standing on the curb. I could hardly look at him because I felt so terrible. "I didn't mean it to happen that way," I said weakly.

Liam nodded. "I know."

"I feel awful," I said.

After a second, Liam smiled. "Well, don't. You won't have any fun if you feel awful. And if you don't have any fun, you won't do a good job with the article. It's the article that's important. Not your feelings or mine."

Liam turned and went back inside. But I couldn't stop feeling guilty. If there were only some way I could make it right. But C.K. was gone and there simply wasn't anything I could do to fix this.

I sighed and shook my head. Liam was right. The article was the important thing. I needed to get started. And I knew just where to begin.

I pulled my cell phone from my pocket and dialed Click Café. My good friend Malcolm Freeman answered.

"Hi, Malcolm, it's Mary-Kate."

"Why are you calling? We don't deliver."

I rolled my eyes. "Just listen. How would you like an enthusiastic waitress for a day—absolutely free?"

"That waitress being you?" he asked.

"That's right!"

"So you're finally going to come around to my side of the counter," Malcolm said. "I know you've been planning to, but all those pesky things like schoolwork and paying jobs kept getting in the way."

"Yeah, my parents are funny about keeping up with stuff like that," I teased back.

I explained about the article.

"You know, Mary-Kate, it's not all glamour here at Click. And I'm not going to let you slide just because we're friends."

"I wouldn't have it any other way," I told him and hung up.

I grinned. My first job for the article was about to happen.

I wondered, though, why Malcolm sounded a little worried.

I shook my head, smiling. *Click just serves coffee. How hard can it be?*

chapter three

"Here it is." I motioned Melanie to follow me down a little side hallway near the management office in the mall on Saturday afternoon.

My heart thumped as I pushed open a big door. Our first trend-spotters meeting! I was psyched. This could be the beginning of something fun—and fabulous!

I gave Melanie a big grin. She gave me a very weak smile. *Oh, well,* I thought. *Maybe once we're in there she'll get excited.*

We stepped into a brightly lit conference room. A long polished table stood in the middle of the room. About a dozen people sat in big comfy chairs around the table. Four were girls our age; the rest were adults. Melanie and I pulled out chairs next to each other and sat down.

"Good morning, girls." Jennifer Lewis smiled warmly at us as she handed us packets. "I think we're all here now. Let's get started."

Ms. Lewis introduced the adults in the group—they were all store owners at the mall and were the judges for the contest. "As for our contestants," she said, "I think you should introduce yourselves."

She turned to the girl sitting next to her. "Louisa, why don't you start us off?"

A dark-haired girl stood up. Her olive complexion was perfect, and so was her outfit. She looked like she was ready to head off to the marina to go yachting. "I'm Louisa Hernandez," she said with a light Spanish accent. "I'm thrilled to be here, and I hope to make you all proud." She sounded very cool and collected—and serious.

When Louisa sat down, a totally Goth girl popped up. "So, I'm Skylar Ives." When she tugged on her shaggy black hair, I noticed every single finger sported at least one elaborate ring. She grinned a black-lipsticked grin. "And in case you didn't notice, my favorite color is black."

Everyone gave a little laugh. Skylar had definitely broken the ice.

"Jodie Greenberg," the next girl said. She wore a tie-dyed peasant top, faded torn jeans, and beads around her neck. Her hair was done in a loose braid with wispy tendrils. Very hippie-retro. "And my mom is amazed that you asked me to be part of this contest. She hates my taste in clothes!"

Another laugh went around the room.

"Mine too!" Skylar said.

The next girl stood up.

"I love all your braids!" Jodie told the girl.

"Thanks." The girl smiled, creating dimples in her smooth, dark skin. She tossed her beaded braids over her shoulder. The movement made her long dangling earrings shake. "I'm Mia Johnson. My favorite looks come from my ethnic heritage. My family is from the Caribbean."

Next came Melanie. She stood up slowly. "I'm . . . uh . . . Melanie Han." She mumbled her last name so quietly I don't think anyone heard her. "And Ashley talked me into this!" She slumped back down into her seat.

No one was quite sure what to make of Melanie's introduction, so I stood up fast. "Hi, everyone. I'm Ashley Olsen, and I think we're all going to have a great time! I can't wait to get started."

"Then let's get to it," Ms. Lewis said. "Now, if you'll open your packets, you'll find all the information you'll need. And we'll all discuss what it is we're looking for."

As we opened our contestant information packets, I glanced around the table at the competition. We all had totally different styles. The judges probably did that on purpose, I thought.

Ms. Lewis passed out a small digital camera to each of us. "These are completely automatic," Ms. Lewis explained. "We're not looking for master photographers here." She smiled reassuringly at us. "The contest is not about the quality of the photos you take; it's about your total presentation."

She explained each of the forms in the packet and instructed us how to begin putting together our photo presentations. Before we knew it, the meeting was over.

Ms. Lewis clapped her hands. "Now, go out there and find the future!"

Everyone scattered. Melanie and I rode the escalator down to the ground floor. I stared at all the people we passed and at the store displays, but I wasn't sure what I was looking for.

"So, what is it that we're supposed to do exactly?" I asked Melanie.

"Spot trends?" Melanie answered. She didn't sound too sure either.

"But what *is* a trend?" I asked. "I mean, how are we going to figure out if what we're seeing is a trend or something silly that will never catch on?"

"I know!" Melanie threw up her hands in frustration. "If you see five people wearing something, does it mean the trend is starting or that it's already over?"

We stepped off the escalator and wandered along the corridor of the busy mall. The other trend-spotters must have had the same idea; we passed by each of them several times.

I thought about some of the things Ms. Lewis had said during the meeting. "A trend isn't just fashion—what designers send down runways," I said. "It's about what's going on in the culture as a whole."

Melanie nodded thoughtfully. "Yeah—like the athletic-clothing thing. The stripes and drawstrings and team-themed clothes that aren't really for working out."

"Exactly!" I nodded. "The clothing trend is part of something larger. It's about how right now there's so much emphasis on health and fitness."

We passed by a line for the movie theater. Melanie stopped and stared at the posters. "You know what else happens? A book or a movie gets really popular, and sometimes it starts a new trend."

I bit my lip. "Except maybe the movie or book was actually *following* a trend," I pointed out. "Not leading it."

We started walking again. "But what about this?" Melanie said. "What if there's a book or movie everybody *thinks* is going to be a big deal but it never catches on." She tugged the ends of her shiny dark hair. "Argh! How can you predict what's going to be a megahit and what's going to tank?"

She made a goofy face, and I laughed at her overexaggerated panic. "This is going to be a real challenge."

I pointed to a bench near a potted tree. "I need to give my feet a break," I told her. We sat down. "You know, I think trend-spotting is sort of an extra sense. You either have it or you don't. Kind of like taste."

Melanie grinned. "Well, we know we both have loads of that!" We high-fived.

We sat a few minutes, studying the crowd. My eyes widened. "I think I've got something."

"What is it?" Melanie asked, excited.

"You know how lots of kids wear team T-shirts or school T-shirts? Well, four guys that work at Click Café just went into the game arcade."

"And?" Melanie asked.

"*And* they're all wearing Click T-shirts even though they're just hanging out."

"You know, I've noticed that, too," Melanie said.

"I wonder if that's a trend," I said. "Job T's replacing school T's."

"Hmmm," Melanie said thoughtfully. "My dad calls things like that 'tribal' fashion."

I was about to snap a photo, when Melanie grabbed my arm.

"Look at her." Melanie pointed to a girl wearing a shirt covered with scribbles peering into a window.

"That pattern looks kind of like graffiti," I said.

"Check out her purse," Melanie said.

"A Chinese takeout box! That is so cute."

Melanie nodded. "She is completely ahead of the curve."

We both lifted our cameras.

"Um, Ash," Melanie said.

"What?" I asked, peering into the camera viewfinder.

"We're both taking pictures of the same girl."

"You're right." I laughed. "That's not what the contest sponsors have in mind."

"Right," Melanie said. She sighed. "I guess we can't be a team."

"It would be more fun if we could be," I said. "But they want six different points of view, not five."

"We need to split up," Melanie said.

"Okay, I'm going to head up this way." I pointed toward the escalator.

"I'll go back the other way and we can—oh, wait." Her eyes widened as she stared over my shoulder. "Hottie alert!"

Before I could turn around, a pair of hands slid over my eyes.

"Guess who?" a voice behind me asked.

"I don't know," I joked. "Oh, wait! Is it my boyfriend, Aaron Moore?"

Aaron laughed. "Good answer," he said, uncovering my eyes. I stood up and gave him a quick hug.

"You will never guess what happened to Melanie and me!" I quickly explained all about the trend-spotter competition.

"That's awesome," he said. "I can't think of two better girls for that gig."

"Speaking of which," Melanie said, standing up, "I'd better get to work!" She waved and hurried away along the crowded walk-way.

"What are you doing here?" I asked Aaron, slipping my hand into his.

"Looking for you," he answered. He squeezed my hand and grinned. "I was hoping you'd feel like going for a drive to celebrate eight whole days of freedom."

"That's sweet," I said. "But I actually have to work." I held up the camera. "There are trends to be spotted!"

Aaron's smile faded. "Oh, well. If you can't . . ." His voice trailed off.

I hesitated. I really did want to get started on my presentation, but I hated disappointing Aaron. Then I realized going for a drive could be a good opportunity to cover a lot more territory.

Besides, I thought, watching Skylar and Louisa head up the escalator, *I want my ideas to stand out. That won't happen if we all look for trends at the mall!*

"That's a great idea." I nodded. "Let's go."

I slid beside Aaron into the front seat of his Dodge Charger and we took off. As we passed by Bennie's Diner, Aaron nudged me. "Check out that paint job." He nodded toward a little black car in the parking lot. It was covered with bright jewel-tone splotches of paint.

"It looks like it's been in a paintball fight!" I said, giggling. "I wonder if that's the next hot thing." I snapped a photo.

We parked the car by Stokers, the video game arcade. As we wandered through the arcade filled with blinking, bleeping, binging games, I noticed several teenagers with little kids in tow.

"Do you think the arcade is becoming a family hangout?" I wondered aloud. "Or maybe a place to bring kids you're baby-sitting?"

"Could be," Aaron said.

After playing several games, we drove near the beach.

"There's a trend for you," Aaron said. He pointed at couple of girls strolling along the sidewalk, one wearing dalmatian-spotted leggings, the other wearing a zebra-striped print shirt. "You could call it 'animal magnetism'!" He grinned at me. "Take a shot of them."

I took the photo even though I knew Aaron wasn't noticing a new trend at all. That look had been around forever. But I wanted Aaron to know I appreciated that he was trying to help.

My head was spinning when Aaron finally dropped me off at home. We'd seen all kinds of people and things that might or might not be new trends. I could barely process all the images whirling around in my brain.

Trend-spotting wasn't as easy as I thought it would be!

chapter four

I couldn't decide if I was more excited or more terrified when I slipped into my seat at the trend-spotters meeting Monday morning. We were making our first presentations to the judges today. I had no idea how mine would stack up against the competition. Was I about to completely humiliate myself?

Jennifer Lewis strolled through the conference room door and smiled. "Okay, let's get started!"

I glanced around the room. Who was going to be first? I hoped it wouldn't be me!

Uh-oh. I just noticed the empty seat. *Where's Melanie?*

I'd spent the whole weekend working on my presentation and hadn't seen or spoken to Melanie. I'd just assumed she was hard at work, like me. *Had she backed out after all?*

I couldn't worry about that now. I had to focus on the presentations.

"Skylar, why don't you go first?" Ms. Lewis said.

"Cool!" Skylar stood up and went to the projector. Ms. Lewis explained how to project her digital photos onto the screen on the wall.

Whew. I'm glad I'm not up first. I took a deep breath to calm my butterflies, then glanced at the door, worried about Melanie. The room went dark, and the first slides splashed on the big screen at the front.

"I figured first time out, I should stick with what I know," Skylar said. Pictures of elaborate Goth jewelry appeared on the screen. "There's a subtle difference in this style now," she explained. "Instead of the antique finish we've seen so far, I've noticed a trend toward pieces with a smooth, shiny finish. Almost as if the look is going futuristic."

"Good eye," a judge said. "I hadn't picked up on that."

The judges scribbled notes, nodding as Skylar flashed through her dozen shots. The room lights came back on.

"It was hard to really see anything in those photos," a judge complained.

"With jewelry, detail is everything," another judge agreed.

Skylar frowned and unloaded her disc.

"Close-ups next time," Ms. Lewis said as Skylar sat back down. Skylar looked discouraged. "All right, who's next? Louisa, are you ready?"

Louisa fumbled with the projector a bit and then started her presentation. The shots were all taken at a stable.

"What you see is a startling shift in color preference," Louisa declared.

I blinked. Startling? I saw a lot of pastel linen and pale cotton twill.

"Uh, as you can no doubt see, there is now a trend toward lighter colors." Louisa tried going to the next photo but kept going backward instead. Ms. Lewis helped her get it straight, and Louisa clicked through her pictures.

"Is this all you have?" one of the judges called out. "It's summer. Everyone goes for lighter clothes during the summer."

"I don't!" Skylar joked. I could tell she was trying to make Louisa feel better.

"Nothing new here," another judge muttered.

Poor Louisa sat down quickly, and Mia stood for her presentation. Despite the tension created by the judges' reactions to Skylar and Louisa, Mia acted completely confident.

Her first photos showed a group of kids whose jeans were patched with brightly colored African print cloth.

"Love the colors," a judge said.

"Great patterns," another commented.

"I thought so, too," Mia said.

One judge shook her head. "It's far too minor a thing to fuss with. It's headed nowhere."

"The trend may not be this specific pattern, but it's part of a larger, more colorful movement," Mia explained.

I was impressed that the judges' comment didn't rattle her. She showed another series of photos of kids who each wore a brightly colored item.

"After neutral tones, camouflage, and"—she smiled at Skylar—"way too much black, I think we're going to see more color." She continued going through her photos. "A little goes a long way. We won't be drenched in color, but it will be used like an accessory."

The judges nodded approval.

"Now that's more like it," one of them said.

"I love the bright bracelets and necklace against the black outfit," another judge added.

Mia beamed as she sat down.

Jodie focused her efforts on boys wearing seventies-style shirts with big collars. "What's next? Wide ties?" one judge said.

"Oh, I hope not," Ms. Lewis said. "But it's great to see what's out there." She smiled warm encouragement at Jodie.

I was the only one left, and was I ever nervous! The judges didn't waste any time on tact if they thought the ideas weren't interesting enough or absolutely cutting-edge. How were they going to respond to my presentation?

I was almost glad that Melanie decided not to come. If she bombed in front of these tough judges, she would be totally crushed. And it would be all my fault, since I dragged her into this, practically kicking and screaming.

I was gathering up my stuff for my presentation, when Ms. Lewis called out Melanie's name.

"Melanie Han?" She looked out at the group gathered in the conference room. It was obvious Melanie wasn't here, but she asked anyway, "Is Melanie Han here?"

I gulped. *Should I make an excuse for Melanie? Figure out something to say so that she wouldn't be disqualified?*

Suddenly the door burst open and Melanie rushed into the room. "I'm so sorry I'm late," she blurted out, dropping her things on the table. She took a few deep breaths. "I decided to make my presentation like a multimedia show," she explained. She was so nervous, her voice shook. "It took longer to burn the CD than I thought it would. Sorry." She reached for her folder, and I could see her hands trembling.

I felt awful seeing her so stressed. I should have just minded my own business, but instead, I had practically forced her to do this. Maybe I wasn't such a good friend after all.

But it became clear there was nothing to worry about.

"Synergy," Melanie declared. She picked up an index card and read from it: "'The interaction of separate items so that the total effect is greater than the individual parts.'" She smiled at the group. "My presentation is called 'Cityscape Synergy.' "

The first shots were of several clay window boxes. Then a close-up of a clay medallion in the center of one box grew across the screen. This was followed by another close-up of an earring cast in a similar medallion pattern.

"You'll see this sort of thing all around you," Melanie said, "if you start looking."

A photo of a flower transformed into a woman's hairstyle that looked just like the petals.

Melanie clicked quickly through a series of photos: an old car with a dented bumper, a group of hip-looking kids standing around it, having fun. Next up was a pair of work boots thrown on top of a trash heap, the toes all dented in and smashed. The toes of the boots echoed the look of the dented bumper, and somehow, the discarded boots looked very, very hip.

"Big or small, synergy is everywhere," Melanie said, clicking for the next photos.

Two photos appeared side by side: one was of jagged light reflecting off a soaring glass skyscraper; the other showed shiny patent leather bags. Melanie had made reflective surfaces suddenly seem trendy.

The lights came up and I realized the judges had not interrupted once. In fact, they were speechless.

"Wow," Ms. Lewis finally murmured, speaking for all of them.

Why had I worried? I knew from the start that Melanie was a natural. I was so happy and relieved, I almost forgot to be nervous about my own presentation, which was next.

When Ms. Lewis called my name, I sucked in a deep breath and stood. I clicked my photos onto the screen.

"These may look like the usual kids in their usual T-shirts. But what you'll see is a new trend starting." I went through the pictures of kids hanging out. "All of these kids have something in common. They're all wearing work clothes—T-shirts, caps, aprons, jackets." I put up pictures of kids at the mall, at the beach, lounging at Click. "And none of them are at work."

I glanced up at my photos. They were clear and showed everyone having fun.

"I love it," a judge said. "It's not a fashion thing—yet. But it's definitely coming."

"With more teenagers working, we'll be seeing more of this," another judge said. "It's a new twist on logos."

I smiled. It felt good to know the judges thought I was actually onto something.

After my presentation, the judges gave some additional pointers about trend-spotting, and then the meeting was over. As we gathered up our things to leave, all of the judges and even some of the other contestants congratulated both Melanie and me. The praise felt good, but what felt best was seeing Melanie holding her head up high.

"I told you that you had the right stuff," I whispered as I squeezed her shoulders. "I am thrilled for you."

"I'm thrilled for you, too," Melanie said. "That tribal thing I told you about worked well for you."

Huh? I wondered if I'd heard wrong, because her comment didn't make any sense. "The tribal thing?" I repeated, a little puzzled by her words. "You gave it a name, but I spotted it. I saw all those work T's around town and went with it."

Melanie smiled. "Of course you did," she said quickly. "And you did a great job with it, too." She patted my shoulder.

Something about her reaction felt, well, patronizing. It was weird. I shook off the uncomfortable feeling.

Melanie didn't mean anything, I told myself. She couldn't have. It was just a remark that came out wrong. Wasn't it?

chapter five

"Mary-Kate," Malcolm drawled, faking patience, "this is a coffee bar. We have one simple job to do—get the right coffee to the right person. And for some strange, unknown reason, it really makes the customers happy if they actually get their coffee while it's still hot."

"I am *so* not in the mood." I glared up at Malcolm from the floor, where I was wiping up a big puddle from the coffee drink I just dropped.

It was probably a good thing I'd dropped it though. I'd way oversweetened *and* overcreamed it.

Being a waitress at Click was turning out to be a lot more complicated than I imagined—certainly nothing like making coffee for C.K. at the magazine office.

"How hard can this be?" I'd asked myself when I first arrived and followed Malcolm around that

Tuesday morning. He had pointed to this nozzle and that bin, explaining what seemed obvious. But after an hour of trying to make sense of the flavor variations and names, I would have demanded a raise—if I hadn't been working for free.

I stood up, remade the coffee drink, delivered it, and wiped up all the spills under the espresso maker. "It looks so easy when you're a customer," I muttered. But the view from the other side of the counter was a whole lot different.

"Hey, everybody, look at the new girl," Brittany said, bursting through the door. Ashley, Aaron, Melanie, and Lauren were with her.

"Is that really you, Mary-Kate?" Lauren asked. "How desperate do you have to be to take a job working for Malcolm?"

"You. Out!" commanded Malcolm, pointing to the door.

Lauren giggled. "You know I'm just joking," she said.

Malcolm raised an eyebrow. "Well, you're on probation." He hurried back to the counter.

"No, seriously," Brittany said, sliding into a booth. "What are you doing here? Don't you already have a job?"

"It's research," I explained, wiping some milk from my chin. "I'm working on an article for *Girlz* magazine about cool summer jobs."

"If she gets through today in one piece," Ashley added, "tomorrow she's going to be a lifeguard." She and Aaron plopped down in the booth opposite Brittany and Lauren. Melanie squeezed in on the end next to Ashley.

"So, how do I look?" I strutted around in a circle to show off my Click uniform and much-too-splattered apron.

"You look great," Aaron said.

"Hey, why don't you tell us about the latest trends in coffee," Ashley said. She grinned at Melanie. "Maybe we'll put it in one of our presentations."

Melanie laughed. "After all, none of us wants to be seen toting around a mug of something that's not totally cool."

"Coffee is not supposed to be cool," Malcolm snapped at me as he slouched past us with another rejected order to replace. "Hot, Mary-Kate. Don't leave it sitting around on the counter while you try to figure out what you're doing."

"If you're in the mood for something chocolate, I love the cocolocomocho," I said, hoping nobody else had heard Malcolm.

The only thing I hate worse than being bad at something is having everyone *witness* me being bad at it!

"But for the absolutely trendiest," I continued, "check out the mocha café à l'orange. It's kind of European and getting really popular." I pulled a pen and pad of paper from my pocket. "So what can I get for you?"

They all called out their orders at once. I scribbled as fast as I could, even though it sounded something like one big strange combination: "Dolce-a-latte-cinna-café-coco-double-breve-espresso-carama-chino-plain-with-two-percent."

It was worse than trying to add and subtract a column of figures in my head with people calling out the numbers at random. I was totally mixed up but didn't want any of them to know.

"Great," I said with a big fake smile. "I'll be right back."

At least, I hoped I would.

"Mary-Kate looks good in her Click outfit," Lauren said as we watched my sister rush off to take care of our orders.

"So what trends did you spot today?" Aaron asked. He knew Melanie and I had had presentations again that morning.

"Actually," I said, turning to Lauren, "you were my inspiration!"

Lauren looked surprised. "Me? How?"

"I remembered your ponytail holders."

Lauren grinned. "Oh, yeah. The twist ties."

"Well, I found other kids who made accessories out of everyday objects," I explained. "I found kids who made earrings out of poker chips and chokers of yarn, and strung bolts or washers on leather cords for a necklace. That kind of thing."

"How fun!" Brittany said. "I'll have to try that."

"What was your presentation about?" Lauren asked Melanie.

"Things that light up," she said. "I showed pictures of shoes with built-in lights that were popular a few seasons ago."

"Then she showed glow-stick jewelry, belts that blinked, PDA's and cell phones that flashed, glowing zippers, earrings, jeans, and blinking baseball caps," I said. "It was great."

"Thanks," Melanie said.

"The judges really liked both of our presentations," I said. I wasn't bragging, I was just really pleased about how well both of us were doing.

"It sounds like you're really having fun," Brittany said.

"Almost too much fun," I admitted with a giggle. "It doesn't feel like a competition or a serious job, but it's both!"

Melanie nodded. "I feel like I'm really on a roll. The ideas just keep coming faster and faster. I can't wait to get started on the next presentation. I already have too many ideas for it."

"Okay, here's your order!" Mary-Kate stood next to our table, holding a tray of whipped-cream-topped coffee drinks. She looked at the tray and then at us. "At least, I *hope* it's your order!"

She placed the drinks in front of each of us, then hurried away again.

I took a sip of my coffee. It wasn't awful, but whatever it was certainly wasn't going to be the next big trend in beverages.

Melanie ignored her coffee and turned to me. "You were right to talk me into this. I think I do have a talent for it."

"That's great." Brittany smiled.

Melanie turned toward Lauren. "You know," she said thoughtfully, "you might want to do something different with your hair."

"What?" Lauren said. She looked surprised.

I stiffened a little. Melanie sounded as if she were criticizing Lauren's appearance.

"Lauren looks perfect all the time," I said, hoping to keep Melanie from hurting Lauren's feelings. Lauren is very sensitive.

"I think that's what's wrong," Melanie said. "She needs to make her look more natural. I think the trend will be away from overmanicured styles."

Lauren's face crumpled into worry. "I don't look natural? That's not good. Is it my makeup? Am I wearing too much?"

"No, no, no," I said quickly. "Your makeup's perfect. *Isn't it, Melanie*." I hoped Melanie would catch the warning note in my voice and reassure Lauren.

But Melanie was too carried away with her own ideas to notice.

She studied Lauren carefully, and it looked as if she were getting ready to express another opinion.

I couldn't let that happen. I accidentally on purpose crashed my coffee into Melanie's.

"Oh, no!" I cried, jumping up. "I'm so sorry!"

"I'll go get some extra napkins," Aaron volunteered. "I don't think we should bother Mary-Kate. She looks kind of busy."

I glanced at my sister. She was cleaning up some coffee of her own at the counter. "Great," I said. "Thanks."

Brittany, Lauren, and I started mopping up the spill while Melanie dabbed at her notebook with her napkin.

"You know, I have so many ideas for the presentation, I'm going to go sit by myself to get some work done," Melanie said.

As soon as Melanie left the booth, I turned to Lauren. "You look fine, really."

Brittany nodded. "Definitely."

Lauren still looked worried. "But why would she say that, then?"

"Melanie's just really worried about this contest thing," I explained. "She'll get over it and turn into her old self again."

At least, I hope *she will,* I thought.

I glanced at Melanie who writing in her notebook. *But it might not hurt to drop a more direct hint,* I decided. Melanie could hurt someone's feelings without meaning to, and I knew she would never want to do that.

Aaron returned with a pile of napkins and I headed over to Melanie's table. She looked up and quickly slapped the notebook shut and slid it into her lap.

I paused. *What is up with that?* I wondered. *Is Melanie worried that I'm going to try to read her notes? She can't think I would copy any of her ideas!*

Does she?

First the "tribal" comment, now this. Then I shook the awful thoughts aside.

No, I'm not going to think like that, I told myself. I was sure Melanie didn't believe I would try to steal her ideas.

"Hi, Melanie," I said. "Can I sit down for a minute?"

Melanie scooted over to make room in the booth, still keeping her notebook under the table. Before I could open my mouth to say anything, she started talking.

"Ashley, I have to tell you that I am totally grateful for your encouragement on this trend-spotting gig. Now that I'm doing it, I really, really love it. I just wanted you to know how much I appreciate what you did to help me."

Wow. Now what? After that speech, I couldn't tell her to stop handing out unwanted advice, or ask her if she imagined I would try to steal her ideas. I felt my mouth opening and closing, but I couldn't make any words come out. I was too confused.

Melanie didn't notice. "You were absolutely right," she went on. "It's in my blood. I have a gift."

She stood up to leave, slipped her notebook into her bag, and slid out of the booth. "Besides," she added with a grin, "it's like you said—what do I have to lose?"

What do I have to lose? Melanie's words echoed gloomily in my head. *How about your friends?*

I seriously began to wonder if this whole trend-spotting thing had been such a good idea after all.

I knew that I had probably completely messed up the coffee orders for my friends. Luckily, they were my friends and didn't make a fuss.

I did better with my next group of customers. I worked really hard to keep all the orders straight. I was finally beginning to get the hang of this thing!

I strolled over to the new customers and took their orders with confidence. One guy wanted the trendy drink I'd told Ashley about: mocha café à l'orange. I strolled back to the counter to fix the drinks.

Uh-oh. "Add one *something* orange syrup." I couldn't quite read Malcolm's scribbles on the instructions he'd taped to the counter above the new fruit-flavored-syrup bottles.

I squinted to read it. One *what*? Cup? Teaspoon? Tablespoon? One squirt? One *what*?

Malcolm was busy on the phone. I didn't want to interrupt him, but I didn't want to wait till he was finished. The coffees were getting cold, and the kids were getting impatient. They kept glancing my way.

A teaspoon maybe? That *had* to be it. A teaspoon was pretty safe—not too much, not too little. Carefully, I measured out a teaspoon of the orange syrup to add to the last coffee order. Then I balanced it on the tray with the others, picked it up, and brought it all over to the customers.

I was halfway back to the counter, when there was a choked explosion behind me. I whirled around and watched the customer with the mocha café à l'orange spit coffee everywhere!

"Ack!" he gagged, holding his throat and making a terrible face. "Water!" he choked out.

"Yuck, gross!" The two girls in the booth jumped up, swatting at the coffee splotches on their tank tops.

"Ewwwwwww, that's disgusting!" the guy yelled. He stood up. "Some water over here, please!"

I scurried back behind the counter as Malcolm dashed across the floor to see what was wrong. Somehow I didn't think the guy would want me to deliver the water.

After a quick conversation with the agitated customers, Malcolm glanced at me, shook his head, then stormed across to where I was cowering behind the counter.

"Café à l'orange," he said, speaking slowly and distinctly as if I were two years old, "is characterized by just the essence, just a *hint*, in fact, of orange flavor."

He handed me what was left of the customer's drink.

"It's *not*, I repeat, *not* supposed to be like getting the *whole blasted orange tree* crammed down your throat!"

I took a step backward. I'd never seen Malcolm so tense. He's the most laid-back guy I know.

"Exactly how much syrup did you put in?" he asked, quieter now.

"I couldn't read your writing," I said, "but now I'm guessing it was less than a teaspoon."

"A *teas*—!" Malcolm yelped. He shook his head. "One drop. One itty-bitty drop. A little goes a really, really long way."

Ooops.

"I'm sorry, Malcolm," I said. "I won't make that mistake again."

"That's good," he said. "Because we'd like to still be in business when this day is over."

I nodded. "Got it."

He handed me a rag. "Now go make nice with those kids so they don't think you were trying to poison them on purpose, okay?"

"Okay, boss."

As I headed back to the table, I glanced over to where my friends had been sitting. *Whew*. I was really glad that they had already left. I shook my head. I had been too busy to notice them say good-bye.

The rest of the day passed in a blur. Since everyone was on spring break, it was one of the busiest days of the year.

I am going to be so nice to every single waitress I see from now on, I vowed silently over and over and over. *And leave big tips, too*, I told myself, picking up three pennies that someone left on the table in one of the booths.

By the end of the day I had finally figured out how to work the espresso machine without getting my feet soaked, and a few customers even complimented me on the coffees I made for them.

"I've seen worse." Malcolm grinned at me as I took off my apron when my shift was done. "Not many, though."

I tossed my dirty apron at him. "Come on, Malcolm, was I really that bad?"

Malcolm caught the apron and dropped it into the laundry hamper. "Once you got the orange-syrup thing straight, things improved dramatically. Actually, I was kind of impressed that you didn't just walk out when things got pretty intense." He grinned. "If the magazine gig doesn't work out, let me know. Maybe we could work something out."

"That's sweet, Malcolm." I laughed. "But after today, I really don't think so. In fact, I don't think I'll ever drink coffee again!"

I called Ashley and told her I was ready for her to pick me up. As I trotted out to the car, I smiled, thinking what an eye-opening story my waitressing experience would make. It occurred to me it would work best if it was written like a slapstick comedy. *Liam is very good at humor writing,* I thought.

I felt a little flicker of guilt again. I'd had all the fun of the actual experience and he was stuck in the office doing the dirty work. He probably spent the day organizing nail polish bottles. He says he's not holding a grudge, I reminded myself.

But was he really telling the truth?

chapter six

"This shouldn't take long," Mary-Kate said as I nosed our pink Ford Mustang into a parking space near the *Girlz* magazine office building. "I've just got to scan in these pictures and type up my notes from today's job at Click Café."

"Take all the time you need," I said. "I'm not in any rush."

I followed her into the building and up the elevator to the magazine office. It should have been empty that late in the day, but someone was still there, hard at work. Liam.

"Are you still here?" Mary-Kate asked him, obviously surprised. "You poor thing."

Liam was sitting on the floor in the crowded little cubicle he and Mary-Kate shared. He held a notebook on his lap and was surrounded by boxes and bins and a hundred little sample-size packages.

"I have to get this done," he said without even looking up. "I seriously can't face another day looking at all these samples, so I'm trying to finish inventorying them and putting them away." He sighed. "Unfortunately, as soon as I get them all logged in, I've still got to write up the blurbs."

He held up a small, brightly colored deodorant stick. "Tell me, Mary-Kate, how can I make stuff like this seem like the absolute latest must-have craze?"

Mary Kate shook her head. "I don't know, but I do know that if anybody can do it, you can, Liam. You really have a gift."

"Hmmmph. Well, flattery will get you everywhere, I guess." Liam smiled.

"I'd help you, but I've got to get these pictures scanned." Mary-Kate looked at Liam, worried.

"It's okay," he assured her. "Go ahead. You've already put in a hard day at Click. I'll be fine. This isn't as bad as it looks."

"If you're sure." Mary Kate scurried out of the tiny office and across the hall to another tiny office, which held the scanner, copier, a computer, and cabinets full of mailing supplies.

"Why don't I help you, Liam?" I offered. I picked up a pen and notebook from the desk. "Maybe it will go faster if you sort and count and I write everything down."

"That would be a lot quicker." Liam nodded. He dumped an armload of sample-size hair conditioners into a clear plastic storage box. "If you want to help, that's great."

Liam called out products and amounts, and I wrote them down in the notebook. I watched the pile of objects grow around him.

So these are the latest hot product lines. I held up a clear-handled toothbrush. Little glittery stars suspended in clear liquid in the handle swirled around like snow in a snow globe. It was so pretty, it actually made me want to brush my teeth.

"I never thought about toothbrush design before," I said, adding the swirly toothbrush to the pile.

"All of these products use style to get your attention," Liam said.

"And who knows," I said, picking up a box containing toilet brushes. "If the design is cool, maybe you'll actually do your chores without complaining so much!"

Liam laughed. "Maybe it's a conspiracy. Parents working with designers to trick their kids into brushing their teeth longer and cleaning the house more often!"

I gestured to the bins stacked around us. "Do you have to write about all this stuff?"

"That's what the companies are hoping," Liam said. "Mary-Kate and I go through the items and pick out anything that stands out. Those are the ones we write up."

"So you're a trend-spotter, too," I said.

Liam shrugged. "Not really. It's more that I look for what was different from last month's shipment. It's C.K. and the other editors who really spot the trends."

"Who knew there was so much going on in the world of toiletries," I said.

"It's big business," Liam said, putting away the bin full of counted toothbrushes. "A big, cutthroat business. Intensely competitive."

"Would it be all right if I borrowed some of these samples?" I asked. "I'd like to use them in my next presentation."

"Sure!" Liam said. "I'd love to hear what the judges and the other trend-spotters think."

"Finished!" Mary-Kate announced. She squeezed back into the office. "How's it going in here?" She shot Liam a worried look.

"Pretty good." Liam stood and stretched. "Thanks to Ashley's help, I should probably be able to get home before dawn."

"Do you want me to stay?" Mary-Kate asked him.

Liam looked surprised. "What? No, no, go home. You have another long day tomorrow."

Mary-Kate bit her lip. "Well, if you're sure."

"Bye, Liam," I said. "And thanks again."

"No, thank *you*!" he answered.

Mary-Kate was quiet as we walked to the car. "So what did you and Liam talk about?" she asked as we climbed into the car.

"We talked about toothbrushes with floaties in the handle, and chore conspiracies. That kind of thing," I answered. I could tell something was bothering her, but I wasn't sure what.

"Did he say anything about . . . me?" Mary-Kate asked.

"About you? No, why would he?" I glanced at her face. "Mary-Kate, are you and Liam . . ."

She laughed. "No, silly, of course not. It's just, well, I'm afraid Liam might be mad at me."

"Mad? Why?" I asked.

Mary-Kate sighed. "C.K. totally misunderstood when we told her our ideas—Liam's ideas, really—for the July issue. She thought *I* was the brilliant one. So Liam is stuck doing boring stuff like sorting lipstick, while I'm out having all the fun."

"Cleaning up spills, getting teeny tips, and putting up with Malcolm's 'I'm the boss' attitude is *fun*?" I asked, surprised. "It looks to me like your contribution to this article isn't exactly going to be a breeze. From what I could tell, you had a pretty rough day today. Maybe Liam got the better deal after all."

"No way." Mary-Kate shook her head. "I had a blast today. Once I got things figured out, it was really fun to get a whole new perspective on things. In fact, I can't wait for tomorrow, when I get to be a lifeguard."

She sighed again. "That's the problem. This article was Liam's idea. He should be the one having fun, not me."

chapter seven

"Trends aren't just found in fashion," I said during my presentation for the Teen Trend-Spotter meeting on Friday morning. "They're all around us if we take the time to look."

I wasn't the least bit nervous now, standing in front of the trend-spotters, Ms. Lewis, and the other judges. No more butterflies, no more sweaty palms. In fact, it felt pretty great to be up there, natural even.

I put up the photos I'd taken of everyday objects: razors in metallic colors, tools with slick handles, animal print mops, plastic storage tubs in fun shapes and sizes, and those glittery toothbrushes with the swirling snowflakes in the handles. I'd scoured hardware stores and toiletry aisles, snapping pictures for today's presentation.

"Sleek designs now give necessities the feel and look of luxury items," I said, clicking through my photos. "If you have a task to do, why not do it with style? This trend is found everywhere, from the most expensive"—I flashed a picture of a gorgeous futuristic car—"to the dime-store stuff." Now I showed a toilet brush with a handle echoing the shiny finish of the car.

"Consumers are demanding the best—but at affordable prices," I continued. "Everything here costs less than twenty dollars." I glanced back up at the screen. "Well," I said, "except for the car, of course." I then showed a picture of a newsstand filled with lifestyle magazines and a list of all the TV shows devoted to home decorating on a budget.

"But this trend isn't all about looks—it's also about how an object feels, how easy it is to use, and how well-designed it is for the human body." Now I showed kitchen utensils with easy-to-grip handles and specially designed desk chairs. "This concern for designing with the human body in mind—ergonomics—will also wind up influencing fashion," I concluded. "I think we'll see it in backpack design, shoes, accessories, and purses. Kids will want to use and wear items that are of good quality, even for the most simple task."

"Very good," Ms. Lewis said as I sat down. "I think I've seen this beginning to come into play." She turned to Melanie. "You're next."

Melanie stood up. "Kid biz," she announced as her pictures flashed on the screen.

"These are teen entrepreneurs," Melanie explained. "Each one of them has gone into business for themselves." She showed photos of a high school guy doing yard work with his own billboard and business cards advertising his yard-work services. Next up were two girls passing out flyers advertising their summer crafts day camp for kids.

"Young people, but grown-up businesses," Melanie said. "And when teens work, they also spend money. I think there will be a trend toward business accessories designed, developed, and priced for teen tycoons."

"Like what?" a judge asked.

Melanie smiled. "Dictaphones built into cell phones. Portable fax/printer combinations and trendy backpacks to carry them in. Printing and design services simplified for busy 'kid-trepreneurs.'"

'Another great buzzword," a judge said. "'Kid-trepeneurs.'"

"Very impressive." Ms. Lewis nodded her approval. The meeting broke up after Melanie's presentation.

"You're so smart," Louisa said to Melanie. "I really wish I had your fashion sense."

Melanie gave Louisa a quick smile and thanked her. But as soon as Louisa was out of earshot, Melanie leaned toward me and whispered, "That poor girl. She really does need some help. Can you believe those twill slacks she is wearing? Ugh! She really could use my advice."

Whoa. I'd never heard Melanie sound so smug before.

"Maybe you ought to wait for Louisa to ask before you go giving her advice," I said as we left the conference room and headed toward the escalators.

Melanie didn't seem to hear the irritation in my voice. "Maybe you're right. But on the other hand, she'd probably be really shy about asking someone like me for fashion help. After all, you heard what the judges keep saying. You and I are turning into top trend-spotters. And of course, I've been around fashion all my life. It just comes naturally to me. That could be intimidating for lots of people."

"Well," I began, but she kept talking.

"Listen, Ashley," she went on, "I really owe you a huge favor for getting me into this contest. So I just want to be sure you know, if you ever want to ask me anything, I hope you won't be shy—or intimidated—about it."

Huh? I couldn't believe my ears. Was she suggesting that I needed fashion help?

Melanie stepped onto the down escalator ahead of me. I quickly slid onto the next step. Melanie rested her hand on the rail and turned to face me.

"You know, when we started this trend-spotting thing, I didn't darc tell my dad about it," she said as we rode down to the main floor. "But yesterday I got up the courage to tell him about the whole thing. He is so proud of me and how great it's turning out for me." She laughed. "It's a brand-new bonding thing we have going between us now." She turned back around and stepped off the escalator.

I was still so stunned, I couldn't speak. I was glad about her father but still really peeved by Melanie's know-it-all tone and weird comment. She glanced at her watch.

"I've got to run. Things to do, trends to spot!" With a wave, she dashed off, swallowed up in the crowd of Friday mall shoppers. I just stood where she'd left me, completely flabbergasted.

I shook my head and decided to slip into a nearby store to cool off. As I passed a mirror at the end of an aisle, I stopped to study myself.

What did Melanie mean? Why does she think I would need her advice? Am I a complete loser in the fashion department?

I shook my head.

No way. There was absolutely nothing wrong with how I dressed or how I looked. *Melanie is nuts.*

I flipped through a rack of summer tops, trying not to slam the hangers in irritation. *What makes you think you're such a fashion genius anyway, Melanie Han? Who died and appointed you the fashion police?*

For one second I wished I'd had the guts to say that to Melanie. That would have put her in her place.

I pulled a camisole top off the rack and studied it, turning it this way and that in the not-so-great mall light. Was it gray? Or blue? Would the color bring out my eyes or wash out my skin tone?

I hung it back up, rattling the other tops on the rack. Melanie would probably say the camisole was totally last year. And since she's the fashion genius around here . . .

Hmmmph. Somebody needs to tell her free advice is worth just what you pay for it. Maybe that would shut her up.

I walked over to a shoe display and picked one up. *When did heels start looking like this? Where have I been?*

Speaking of heels . . .

I chewed on a cuticle, so absorbed in my growing resentment at Melanie, I didn't even care about the damage I was doing to my fingers. All that I could focus on was how awful Melanie was becoming, and all the snappy, clever comebacks I could have said in response.

Maybe I should have said those things, I thought. *Maybe Melanie needed to hear them.*

But even though I was angry and a little hurt, I didn't want to be mean. And anything I said to Melanie right now *would* be mean.

I'm just going to have to keep my mouth shut for a while, I told myself. Until I could think of a nice way to help Melanie understand that she needed to back off with her advice, I wouldn't say anything at all. Otherwise, I'd be just as bad as she was.

As I walked out of the store, I caught another glimpse of my reflection in a full-length mirror. I hesitated in front of it. *Maybe I have been fooling myself all these years,* I thought. *Maybe Melanie is right and I could use her tips.*

Melanie has been around fashion all of her life—it makes total sense that she'd turn out to be a natural trend-spotter. And me? I gave myself a long, hard look in the mirror. Am I just kidding myself? Am I totally out of my league in this contest?

I turned away quickly and hurried out of the store. All of the clever, witty things I was going to say to Melanie went right out of my head. All I wanted to do was go home and change!

"You must be Mary-Kate Olsen." The lady at the Malibu Beach Club front desk smiled at me. "I need to get a copy of your Red Cross lifesaving certificate for our records."

I pulled the card out of my purse and handed it to her.

"Thank you," she said. "I'll go make a copy and bring it right back. Meanwhile, why don't you go change in the locker room, then have a seat right there."

She pointed to a comfy couch and chairs in the lounge area, where several impossibly tanned surfer-type, drop-dead-cute lifeguard trainees were hanging out. I was surprised to see that I was the only girl. "Class will be starting in a few minutes. I'll tell Jon you're here."

"Great!" I hurried into the pristine changing room. I had already done a mini-tour of the club and could not believe my good luck. *This place rocks!*

I opened the locker and found the bright pink flip-flops and luxurious plush towel provided by the club. I wiggled my hips and pumped my arms, doing a mini-victory dance. Then I blushed and glanced around. Luckily, the locker room was empty!

I changed into my swimsuit, shoved my clothing and purse into the locker, and hurried back out to the main area. I had to force myself not to gape as I took in the gorgeous surroundings—the beautiful, "under the sea" tiles on the walls, the sleek reception area and lounge, the open-air deck, the Olympic-size swimming pool sparkling outside in the sunshine.

And on top of all that, I get to spend all day with these incredible hunks! I sat down next to a blond guy with great hair and even greater abs. *Keep your mind on the article,* I reminded myself.

Jon, the instructor, appeared. He was in his twenties, seriously tan, and well built. He wore a Malibu Beach Club T-shirt and trunks, and a whistle hung around his neck.

"This way, gang!" He beckoned us to follow him. I got up, trailing the rest of my classmates down a hall that led out to the pool area. Before we got outside, however, Jon stopped us, pointing to a series of large photos mounted on the wall.

"Take a good look at these kids," Jon told us. "Every one of them was saved from drowning right here at this club—saved by lifeguards just like you."

I nodded. Lifeguarding was an awesome, important responsibility.

"These pictures remind us why we're here," Jon said. "It's hard work, but it's important work. And I think you're going to enjoy it."

We lined up alongside the pool. "First, warm-up laps!" Jon said. "To be a good lifeguard, you need to be in extremely good shape."

No kidding, I thought, secretly eyeing Jon. He blew his whistle and we all dove in.

After we'd each completed ten laps and some aquatic exercises, Jon blew his whistle again. We climbed out of the pool to learn rescue techniques.

"We're going to work these holds here on the deck," he explained. "Then we'll get into the water and put them into practice. So pair up."

The hunk to my left turned and faced me. I gazed into a pair of warm brown eyes, topped by soaking wet curls. "Hi," he said. "I'm Brendan. Should we be partners?"

"Sure," I told him, hoping my wet hair was as flattering as his. "I'm Mary-Kate. And I promise to try not to drown you!"

Brendan and I worked together the rest of the morning. Jon kept us so busy, I nearly forgot that I was surrounded by a dozen of the most incredible-looking guys I'd ever laid eyes on.

Almost.

After a full morning of rescues, and then timed laps, we broke for lunch, catered by the club. I nibbled at a fresh fruit salad, gazing happily out toward the beach.

What an assignment, I thought, sighing with pleasure. All of the exercise and concentration energized me—I felt totally pumped.

Then I remembered Liam, stuck in that tiny office while I was out here in the glorious sunshine having a great time. Guilt soured my stomach, and I tossed my uneaten salad away.

"Break's over!" Jon announced.

You can't think about Liam, I told myself. *You have to stay focused on today's assignment*.

Next up was classroom work, then sprints on the beach, and finally back to the pool for more practice rescues. My partner this time was a totally hot guy with spiky black hair named Alan.

"I don't know, Mary-Kate," he teased me. "With you as lifeguard, I think I'd pretend to drown all day just to get you to rescue me!"

I laughed and splashed water at him. "Then I guess I'd better learn what I'm doing!"

Just as I thought my arms and legs would give out and that my fingertips were permanently pruned, Jon blew his whistle.

"Great job, everyone," he called, clapping his hands. "We'll call it a day."

"Wow," I said to Alan. "The sun is starting to set."

"Time flies, right?" he said, grinning.

"Exactly."

Even though I was exhausted, I was sorry the training session was over. It wasn't just the gorgeous guys all around me. I loved how my muscles felt after so much exercise, and, more important, the idea that I would have the skill to save lives was exhilarating.

I followed the rest of the trainees back to the club. At the door, I took one last, longing look at the pool area and the shimmering beach beyond it.

I turned to step inside, when Jon touched my arm. "Hang on, Mary-Kate. I want to ask you a question."

"Sure," I said, tossing my towel over my shoulder.

"You were definitely one of my star pupils today," Jon said, smiling. "You're a strong swimmer, you caught on really quickly to everything we went over today, and you're already certified. You probably have the most potential in the whole class."

I tried not to blush at the praise. "Wow. Thanks!" I said. "All I know is, I had the best time today. I'm sorry it's over."

"It doesn't have to be over," Jon said, folding his arms across his tanned chest. "I know this was supposed to be a one-shot deal for the magazine. But I was wondering if you'd be interested in working here for the whole summer. We've got a few slots to fill, and I would be really pleased if you'd consider applying for one of them."

My jaw dropped and I stared at Jon. "Are you serious?"

He smiled. "Completely."

Apply for a job here? Work here every day, hang out in the sunshine, at this awesome club, with all those ultracute, totally hunky guys? I was absolutely stunned.

Then I bit my lip. I already *had* a job—at *Girlz* magazine—and it was supposed to last all summer. I'd already committed, and the truth was, I loved it.

"I'm sorry, Jon," I said, hearing the disappointment in my own voice. "I don't think a job here will be possible."

"Oh, well," Jon said. "If you change your mind, give us a call, okay?"

"Okay."

He hurried back inside, and I turned and stared at the pool again. I slowly began to rub my hair with the towel.

You did the right thing, I told myself. *The job at* Girlz *is a dream job. I'd be totally stupid to even think about taking this lifeguard job when it meant I'd be giving up the job of a lifetime.*

I shook my head and wrapped the towel around my shoulders. *This is a total no-brainer.*

Isn't it?

Then why couldn't I stop thinking about it?

chapter eight

I decided to stop in at Click Café to get some coffee. Since Mary-Kate wouldn't be working there, I knew I'd get what I'd ordered!

The place was packed, but I spotted several friends from school already clustered along the coffee bar. I went over to sit with Brittany, Lauren, and some other girls we knew—Cammy Tilton and Heather French from social studies, and Tori Swanson, who was in our drama class.

They were all fuming.

"Wow, guys, what's wrong? You all look as if you're having a really bad day," I said as Heather and Cammy slid over to make room for me to sit with them.

"Well, Ashley, I am apparently having a bad *hair* day." Brittany scowled and rolled her eyes.

"At least, that's what Her Majesty the Queen of Fashion thinks."

"Melanie?" I groaned with an awful sinking feeling.

Brittany nodded, rubbing a hand over her short, tight curls. "According to her, I have a bad- hair day every day of the week. My hair is, quote, hopeless."

Melanie strikes again! "There's nothing wrong with your hair," I assured her.

"If you ask me," Heather said, "our little fashion cop is taking this whole 'I'm a trend-spotting genius' thing too far."

"Ashley, be honest." Tori leaned in close to me. "Do I look like a total train wreck? I thought I looked fine when I left home this morning. But maybe I'm one of the fashion clueless and always get it wrong." She shook her head. "After what Melanie said, I feel horrible." She sat straight up. "How do I leave the house looking so stupid every day." She moaned.

"You don't look stupid," Heather said, then added softly, "At least, *I* don't think you do. But what do I know?"

I frowned. This was getting out of hand in a big way. Melanie had *everybody* second-guessing themselves now. Not just me. I'd been so rattled by Melanie's comment, I'd changed my outfit five times that morning!

"What else did Melanie say?" I asked, almost afraid to hear the answers.

"Well," Lauren said, "she told me, 'Whatever kind of look you were going for, you missed,' among other things."

"Melanie said that my outfit is 'so last week,'" Cammy said. "I just spent all my babysitting money on these jeans. Now what am I supposed to do? And she had the nerve to tell me not to bother donating them to charity because even they wouldn't want them."

Yikes. Melanie was outdoing herself.

"Melanie's just trying to be helpful," I said, even though I knew it probably wouldn't make them feel any better.

"Oh, sure." Tori nodded. "Melanie's actually really nice—until she opens her mouth."

Heather grinned. "Melanie reminds me of someone—and I don't like *her* either."

Now everyone was laughing, trying to think of mean things to say about Melanie.

"You know what Melanie is turning into?" Brittany said, jumping into the put-down party. "She's become 'The Fashionator.' And I think it's time something is done about her."

She put down her coffee and stood up. Her brown eyes glinted, and I could tell she was ready to find Melanie and read her the riot act.

I jumped up and put my hand on Brittany's arm to stop her. "No, I'll talk to her." I looked around the circle of my friends, feeling really bad. "It's my fault you guys got fashionated. Somebody needs to tell her to back off, and I think it ought to be me."

"How is it *your* fault that Melanie is turning into a one-girl fashion police force?" Heather asked.

"It's the contest," I explained. "She didn't want to do it. Then—brilliant me—I kept telling her how she was perfect for it. Now I wish I hadn't pushed so much."

"Me too," Brittany said.

"Honestly, she thinks she's doing everybody a favor," I told my friends. "She doesn't realize she's hurting people. If I tell her how she's upsetting everyone, I'm sure she'll understand." I looked at Brittany. "Okay?"

Brittany hesitated, then sat back down. "All right. But if you need any help, just give me a yell. I'll be happy to back you up." She smirked. "Although I can promise you, it won't be pretty."

Ouch. I winced. *If Brittany finds Melanie before I do . . .*

"I'll see you all later." I excused myself and headed to the door to do serious damage control.

Melanie wasn't hard to find—she was just a couple of blocks down from the café, looking in shop windows, her notebook in hand.

"Hi, Ash." She smiled, quickly flipping her notebook shut. "What do you think—is that yellow belt hoping to start a trend or is it just plain ugly!"

I glanced at the window display. Melanie was right. The belt *was* awful.

"I didn't come here to trend-spot, Melanie. The truth is, there's something I have to tell you."

"Really?" Melanie's eyebrows shot up when she heard the warning note in my voice.

"I know you're trying to be helpful when you give people fashion pointers and criticize their hair and clothing," I began.

She nodded. "You're the one who told me I have a talent, remember? I'm glad I can use it to help people."

"It's not helping people, Melanie," I explained. "It's hurting their feelings. Nobody likes to be told they look stupid or out-of-date or have bad hair or got their makeup wrong. It doesn't really matter *why* you're saying it if it still hurts."

"Do you think I should go around lying to people?" Melanie asked.

"No, but you could try saying something nice. Or maybe don't say anything instead of saying something that might be hurtful."

Melanie walked toward the next window, so I followed her. "Why are you making such a big deal out of this, Ashley?" she asked. "I'm just telling the truth to help people. Nobody should be offended about that."

She just wasn't getting it at all. It was as if she couldn't hear what I was saying. "I think you're taking this all just a little too seriously," I said.

She turned around to face me. "And I think," she said, "that you're so concerned about the contest, you have forgotten all about friendship. In fact, you're so worried about winning that you're willing to cheat."

"What?" My mouth dropped open. I couldn't believe what I'd just heard. "What are you talking about?"

Melanie crossed her arms over her chest, looking smug. "I heard Mary-Kate talking about how you dropped by the magazine and helped out with the product samples. That's where you got your 'fun fashion' trends presentation, isn't it? You swiped it from the magazine article they were working on."

I was completely stunned. I stood staring at Melanie until I could finally speak. "You are totally out of line," I sputtered. "You are so wrong! Not only about that, but about the whole silly contest. I really don't care who wins. The idea was to have fun."

"No, it's not," Melanie said. "Right from the start, it was all about winning. That's why you pushed so hard for me to enter, isn't it? You wanted to show me up. And now you're trying to turn everybody against me."

I shook my head. "I can't believe I'm hearing you say that! Why would you even think such a thing? Listen to yourself!"

Melanie just smirked.

I took in a deep breath, trying to calm down. "Melanie, normally you are one of the nicest people I know. But all of a sudden, here you are, going around saying mean things and making people mad. What is wrong with you?"

"Nothing's wrong with me. I'm just right, is all. And none of you can stand it."

I looked her straight in the eye. "No way. In fact, you're dead wrong. Wrong about the contest, wrong about the magazine, wrong about 'helping' people. All you're doing is making everybody unhappy and angry. In fact, they're actually calling you the Fashionator."

Oops. I hadn't meant to say *that*.

I thought she would be upset, but Melanie just shrugged. "So what. They're just jealous. And so are you."

She whirled around and stalked away. I gaped after her for a moment, and then walked in the opposite direction. I didn't want to risk running into her.

"I tried to help," I muttered. "I tried to be nice. But she just wasn't interested."

Great, I thought. *Now Melanie has me so upset that I'm talking to myself*.

I stomped home, wondering how to handle the situation.

There was only one thing to do—beat the pants

off Melanie in the competition. Show her she's not the only one who knows what she's doing. Then she'll have to admit she's been wrong.

There was only one problem.

How was I going to win?

chapter nine

"Thanks for coming along to take photos, Ashley," I said. I hooked leashes on Mutt and Jeff, two sleek greyhounds I was preparing to walk. That was today's job—dog walker. I had picked a trail that wound through a shady neighborhood park.

"At Click and at the pool there were always people around to take pictures." I grinned down at the dogs. "I don't think these pooches could handle the camera for me."

"No prob, Mary-Kate," Ashley said. She aimed the camera she used for trend-spotting at the dogs. "I just hope the pictures don't come out all blurry!" She laughed as Mutt and Jeff tangled me up in their leashes. "Those dogs don't want to stop moving!"

I freed myself from the dog leashes. "They won't be like this the whole time," I said, though I wasn't exactly sure if that was true. "Besides, Liam is a whiz with the computer—he can fix any little problems with the pictures after we upload them."

The two dogs pulled us along at a steady pace. They were pretty well behaved, only occasionally veering off the path.

"They're probably picking up the scents of other dogs that are walked in the area," I said.

Ashley ran ahead on the path and turned around. "Let me take a picture. You're framed really nicely by the low branches of that tree."

I tugged on the dogs' leashes, getting them to stop. "Look pretty at the camera," I said to them. I smiled at Ashley and she took the shot.

"Great." She bent down and patted Jeff. "You're so photogenic," she told the dog.

I gazed down at the pair of slim gray dogs and grinned. "Hey, don't they look like fashion models?"

Ashley stood back up and laughed. "Especially those long legs. They'll be knockouts in your magazine!"

I giggled. "Maybe we could—yikes!" I struggled to hang on to the leashes as the dogs suddenly bounded along the path. "Ashley!" The dogs took a sharp turn and dragged me into the underbrush and through the woods. "Ashley, help!"

I could hear Ashley behind me, crashing through the bushes, trying to catch up. "Mary-Kate!" she called.

"Mutt! Jeff! Slow down!" I shouted. But the dogs ignored me. *What has you so excited*? I peered through the foliage and realized there was a rabbit scurrying up ahead of us.

"So that's it," I said, tugging hard on the leashes. "You leave that rabbit alone."

As if they understood me, they suddenly raced back onto the path. I stumbled after them, hoping they'd slow down. *No wonder greyhounds are racing dogs*, I thought. *They have serious speed*.

"Mary-Kate!" I heard Ashley shout behind me. "Where are you?"

"I don't know!" I hollered back. "Just follow my voice!"

The dogs came to such a sudden stop, I nearly tripped over them. "What?" I asked them. "Finally got tired?" I took several deep breaths. "Oh, I see, you found a friend," I said, watching the dogs sniff a beautifully clipped poodle—who was being walked by an amazingly cute guy.

"Hi! Sorry!" I gasped, still trying to catch my breath. I hoped my hair wasn't a total mess from my mad dash through the woods.

"Hi," he said, giving me a killer smile. "Looks like your dogs are the friendly type."

"And your dog is gorgeous!" I said, hoping my charges would stay under control.

"Thanks." He looked down at Mutt and Jeff. "Those greyhounds are really beautiful," he said. "Are you thinking of competing them?"

"Oh, they're not mine," I said. "I'm just walking them."

"There you are!" Ashley called. She raced over to join us. "Who's your new friend?" she asked.

"I don't know, actually," I said with a smile.

He laughed. "Oh, sorry, I'm Dan, and this pretty lady at my feet is Mystic Splendor's Lassie. But I just call her Missy."

"I'm Mary-Kate, and this is my sister, Ashley," I said. I nodded toward the greyhounds. "And this is Mutt and that's Jeff. No fancy names for these dudes." I giggled. "They're not well mannered enough to deserve them."

"Well, you chose excellent clients." Dan rubbed Mutt on the top of the head. "Hey, if you like dogs, you should meet some of my friends. We meet in the same spot most days while we're all out walking our dogs."

"Great," I said, carefully pulling Mutt and Jeff away from the poodle. "This will give me more information for the article." I explained about the *Girlz* magazine article I was researching as we walked with Dan back down the trail.

"Wow," Ashley said as she came around a bend in the path. "Those are some spectacular dogs." She quickly began snapping photos of dogs and their owners lounging on the benches that overlooked a little stream running around the perimeter of the park.

"They're show dogs—most of them, anyway," Dan explained. "We compete in shows all up and down the coast. Even people who don't enter their dogs come along. It's kind of an all-consuming hobby for some of us. In fact, there was a show this morning."

Mutt and Jeff waded into the center of the little huddle of dogs, sniffing, wagging their tails, and quivering, checking everybody out.

I looked around the group, trying to figure out why the scene seemed slightly, well, odd. Then it hit me. "It's true," I whispered to Ashley, who was taking pictures. "People really *do* look like their dogs."

"They're all so . . . so . . ." Ashley said, trying to come up with the right word.

"So well groomed?" I said.

"Exactly!"

Even the dogs that were mutts were clipped and snappily styled. In fact, it was hard to say who was more carefully groomed, the pets or their owners!

"Mary-Kate is writing an article about different kinds of jobs," Dan explained.

"Today I'm focusing on professional dog walkers," I said, taking my notebook and pen out of my backpack. "Has anyone here done that?"

Dan's friends were a gold mine of great quotes for the article, and Ashley took loads of photos. I glanced at my watch and realized we had to get my charges back to their owners.

"Come on, Mutt, Jeff," I said, shaking their leashes to get their attention. "Time to go home!"

Whoa! Mutt suddenly took off, tearing across the path and back into the woods.

"Oh, no!" Mutt dragged me, I dragged Jeff, and all the other dogs took off, yanking their leashes out of their owners' hands to follow us.

I tried not to trip over dogs and leashes as I struggled to rein in Mutt and Jeff, but their excitement and their combined strength was more than mine. I could barely keep up!

"Stop," I gasped over and over.

Several of the dogs' owners were desperately grabbing at the leashes as they ran. Dan managed to snag two halfway down the hill, another guy had one, and two girls caught three dogs between them. I couldn't stop Mutt and Jeff, though.

We crested a hill, then sped down the other side. *Oh, great.* We were headed straight for the pond.

Looks like I'm going for a swim, I realized. I hit the water's edge running, tripped, and fell flat on my face, the leashes still clutched tight in my hands.

The dogs dragged me a few feet, but soon the water got too deep for them to keep running and they slowed down. I stood up, sputtering, and wiped the water from my face.

I glared at Mutt and Jeff, who didn't seem too happy to be in the pond. "Don't look at me," I scolded them. "This swim wasn't my idea."

I trudged back to the water's edge with the dogs in tow. Ashley, Dan, and two of Dan's friends grabbed the dogs by their collars and held them tight.

"Oh, Mary-Kate, are you all right?" Ashley asked.

A red-headed girl peeled off her cardigan. "Here," she said, draping it around my shoulders. "Don't want you to freeze."

I was so embarrassed, I could hardly look at them. I was clumsy, soaked, and muddy, while they were all combed, fluffed, and polished. *I bet none of their well-mannered dogs ever dragged any of them into a pond*.

"I can't believe you did that," I scolded Mutt and Jeff, afraid to look at anybody else. "Naughty dogs."

"We'd better get you home quick," Ashley said, taking one of the dog's leashes and making certain I had a tight grip on the other.

I nodded. I wanted to get out of sight, and get changed and dry. "I'm so sorry," I told Dan and his friends. "Are the dogs okay?"

The girl who'd given me her sweater laughed. "They're fine. Besides, it was good for all of us, probably the best exercise we've had all week."

"I'm glad all of you managed to catch your dogs before they wound up in the pond, too," I said, grateful they weren't mad at me. "I'd better get these troublemakers home quick or I'll be in real trouble."

"Maybe we'll see you out here again sometime soon," Dan said. "We're all here every day."

"I'll definitely drop by to say hi," I said. I smiled at the red-haired girl. "And to return the sweater." I nodded toward Mutt and Jeff. "But don't worry, I won't be bringing these two characters with me."

Ashley and I said good-bye, then headed for home.

"Please tell me you got some good pictures," I begged Ashley as we left the park. "Before the pond incident, I mean. I don't think I could stand it if this was a total waste."

"I think I have plenty," Ashley said. "Did you get some helpful information?"

"Definitely," I answered. "Except for that surprise dunk in the pond, walking dogs could be a great job. It's perfect if you like animals and you enjoy meeting people."

Ashley nodded. "I guess dogs are great conversation starters. It's really easy to talk to complete strangers when you have something like dogs in common."

"Dan said he's even met people who walk dogs belonging to all kinds of famous people!"

"I wonder if those pets look like their owners!" Ashley laughed. "Just imagine!"

We dropped off the dogs at their house. "Do you want to come with me while I walk the next dog too?" I grinned at her. "I'm hoping it will go more smoothly."

"Sure," Ashley said. "It's a gorgeous day—it will be nice to spend it outside." She sighed. "It will also give us a chance to catch up. We've both been so busy these past few days, we haven't had any time to talk."

"That's true," I said. From her tone I could tell she had something on her mind. "Is something up?"

Ashley bit her lip. "Well, I have been dying to talk to you. I've got a problem and I need your advice."

"Me too," I said. "I've got a tricky situation of my own to sort out."

"All right," Ashley said. "You first."

As we drove over to the next dog-walking job, I filled Ashley in about the lifeguard position Jon had asked me to consider.

"That's a toughie," she said, frowning. "Let me think about it."

"Okay," I said. I felt better now that I'd told her. Talking things over with my sister always helped, even if we didn't come up with a solution right away. "So what's bothering you?" I asked as I parked the car.

She let out a long sigh, then told me about Melanie's changed attitude, and how she was alienating all of our friends.

"I think you're right, Ash," I said, shaking my head sympathetically. "It really is up to you to somehow help her get the message. And hopefully, without destroying your friendship."

"Isn't it funny how complicated our lives got during spring break?" Ashley laughed. "Most people take advantage of a school holiday to relax and regroup and just have a good time."

I hugged her back. "We'll work this all out," I told her. "We always do. You'll see."

chapter ten

The day finally came. I sat in the conference room waiting to hear the judges' choices for the Teen Trend-Spotter finalists.

I glanced at Melanie. *This should have been an exciting day for us to share,* I thought. *Instead, we're barely speaking.*

"You've all done a marvelous job," Jennifer Lewis said as she stood at the head of the long table. "So give yourselves a big hand."

We all smiled as we applauded. I could see everyone at the table was nervous. Just like me.

"If it were up to me," Ms. Lewis continued, "I'd name each of you as a finalist. Unfortunately, we had to narrow it down to two. But we do have a gift for each of you to show our appreciation for your participation."

One of the other judges got up and passed out colorful gift bags with big bright bows to each of us. I forced myself not to peek inside as we waited for the final announcement.

"It was a difficult decision, as you all can imagine," Ms. Lewis said. "Your presentations were so well done, so inventive, and truly impressive. I want to thank each of you for all your hard work."

I crossed my fingers under the table for luck.

"The hard work isn't over for the finalists, though," Ms. Lewis said. "To determine the winner, each finalist will design a display for the front windows of Glitter and Glam."

Wow. That's going to be some challenge, I thought. I felt a tiny flutter of nerves, wondering if being a finalist would be such a great thing!

Ms. Lewis smiled broadly. "And now let's congratulate Melanie Han and Ashley Olsen, our two finalists."

There was a round of applause while I let out my breath and uncrossed my fingers. *I really did it!* I thought.

"Congratulations!" I whispered to Melanie.

She ignored me.

Fine, I thought. *Be that way*.

We all said good-bye, and then Ms. Lewis brought us outside the store to show us which Glitter and Glam windows we would be designing to determine the winner.

Melanie studied her window for half a second, then started scribbling in her notebook.

I will absolutely positively not let her see me fumble, I vowed silently. I pulled out my notebook and pen from my backpack. I tried to look completely poised and assured as I scribbled in my own notebook, hoping I looked like I had a couple of dozen truly spectacular ideas.

I felt someone standing behind me, and then someone said, "A, B, C, D, E, F, G, H, I . . ."

I whirled around.

"Ashley, why are you speed-writing the alphabet?" Aaron asked.

I peeked at Melanie, hoping she didn't hear him. No such luck. She was smiling smugly.

I gritted my teeth.

"What's wrong?" Aaron asked, puzzled. "I thought you'd be happy to see me. But you don't look very happy."

"I need a pretzel," I said. I pulled him toward the kiosk and out of earshot of Melanie.

"Did I say something wrong?" Aaron asked.

"It's not your fault." I sighed. "It's just that Melanie and I have been having some . . . issues."

"Issues?"

"Yes, issues. This competition has really gone to her head. She's convinced she is smarter than everyone else, and she's gotten way too generous with her advice."

"Hmmmm." Aaron nodded. "That explains some things I've heard."

I groaned. "See? It's getting way out of hand. Things are so tense now between Melanie and me that I'm afraid we might not even be friends anymore." I shook my head. "I almost wish we never got picked to be trend-spotters."

"You don't really mean that, do you?" Aaron asked.

I shrugged. "At first I thought it was so cool that we were chosen. But it's not so cool now that I see what it's done to us."

I looked over at Melanie again. She was hard at work, sitting on the floor, sketching in her book.

I shook my head mournfully. "This competition has been fun, but it's not at all worth losing a friend over. And I'm afraid I have."

"Wow, Liam, you are totally amazing!"

I looked around our completely reorganized little cubicle at *Girlz* magazine. While I'd been out serving coffee, chasing dogs, and saving cute boys from drowning, Liam had streamlined our office, stored all the bins, cleaned up my disjointed notes, organized them into a detailed outline for the article, plus sorted and indexed my photos. And that was all on top of the progress he was making on the product-samples article!

I didn't know what to say. He'd gone way beyond the call of duty.

"You didn't have to do all this," I said, feeling more guilty than ever.

"Are you kidding? I love doing this stuff." Liam beamed. "I feel energized. Our article is shaping up really well. Better than I'd hoped."

He called the layout up on the computer screen. "Check this out," he said. I watched his face light up as he explained how he thought we should place the photos and captions, where the bullets and sidebars would go, the estimated word count, everything.

I wished I could be as enthusiastic as he was about the details. But I just couldn't stop thinking about the beach club job offer.

"What do you think of this arrangement?" Liam asked.

I snapped back to reality. *Focus*, I told myself. *This is your job. So do it*.

"That looks good," I said. "But what if we moved some of the text here?"

"That could work." Liam hit some keys, playing with the layout.

He called up the files from the lifeguarding gig. "These are great pictures," Liam said. He scrolled through the shots of the training session. "Wow! That looks pretty demanding," he said. He shook his head. "I don't think I could do that."

I felt my cheeks flush from the compliment. "It wasn't such a big deal," I said.

The truth was, I couldn't do what he was doing. Sure, I could put in long, tedious hours on someone else's work—but I couldn't do it cheerfully and enthusiastically. I wouldn't be energized by organizing files and fixing someone else's grammar like he was.

"Liam, I . . ." I wanted to tell him how great I thought he was, but the phone rang, interrupting me.

Liam handed me the phone. "Jon, from the Malibu Beach Club," he said, turning his attention back to the computer.

"Hello?" Why would he be calling me?

"I've just come from a meeting where we screened the job applicants, Mary-Kate," Jon said. "We've filled all the positions but one, and I'm offering you the last slot. But I have to have your answer by the end of the day tomorrow. There are a couple of other people who'd really like the job, and I have to let them know. So get back to me as soon as you can, okay?"

"Sure, Jon. Thanks."

I hung up the phone, more confused than ever. What was I going to do?

"Have you seen anything interesting yet, Ashley?" Aaron asked. We were walking along a little side street near the pier, which was crammed with shops. I was desperately looking for something, *anything*, that might trigger ideas I could use for my window display.

So far, though, I was coming up completely empty.

"Absolutely nothing!" The big day was tomorrow, and my mind was a total blank. I didn't have a single idea, not even a *lame* one.

"It's like the harder I try, the more my brain shuts down." I moaned. "I think I'm starting to panic."

"Don't panic," Aaron said. "You need to relax and have fun with this. It's not something to freak out over. After all, who really cares what's hot and what's not?"

"Who cares? Who *cares*?" I couldn't believe my ears. I stopped in my tracks. "Don't you get that this is not about what's hot and what's not?"

"It's not?" Aaron looked totally confused. "What is it about, then?"

"It's about me, about whether I can pull this off or not."

"Huh?" Aaron looked at me blankly.

"It's about me and pushing myself, whether I can use my brains, my instincts, try something new and not crash and burn."

Aaron grinned. "Oh. I guess I was really misinformed. I definitely had the wrong idea. I thought you just wanted to win."

"I do want to win—but not just for the sake of winning." I sighed. "I'm doing this for a lot of reasons."

He took my hand. "I understand," he said, and I could tell he really did. We kept on walking.

"Look, isn't that Brittany and Lauren?" I pointed across the street where they had just stepped out of a beachwear shop.

I really needed a break to clear my head. "Let's go say hi," I said. We quickly crossed the street to join them.

"Hi," I greeted them. "Are you finding anything good?"

Lauren pulled a pair of frilly flip-flops out of her bag. "Aren't these the coolest!" She giggled as she showed them to me. "I just had to have them."

I had to agree, they were pretty cute.

"Maybe you could use them in your window?" she suggested, obviously hoping to be helpful.

"I don't know," I said. I didn't want to hurt her feelings by telling her the style wasn't new or cutting edge.

"How is the window going?" Lauren asked. "Isn't the final judging coming up really soon?"

I nodded. "It's tomorrow," I said, trying to pretend I wasn't worried.

Brittany frowned. "I heard Melanie's dad just got back from Milan with all kinds of great stuff Melanie ordered for her window."

Great.

I gritted my teeth in frustration. *Melanie will have tons of totally hip stuff straight from Europe to put in her window display and I don't even have a single window-worthy idea.*

"What's your window going to be about, Ashley?" Lauren asked. "Do you have any ideas?"

"It's a surprise," I answered. *Yeah,* I thought. *It's a surprise, all right. It's even a surprise to me.*

Aaron could see how miserable I was and tried to change the subject. "Don't you have to go pick up Mary-Kate from the magazine pretty soon?" he reminded me.

I looked at my watch. It was still a little early, but maybe the drive would clear my head.

We said good-bye to Brittany and Lauren and turned around, walking back down the street to the parking lot.

"Thanks for the bailout just then," I told Aaron when we got to the car. "And thanks for trying to help."

"I wish it had turned out to be more productive," he said. "But something will come to you, I know it will."

I sighed. I wished I was that confident.

After I dropped off Aaron, I drove over to pick up Mary-Kate with the top down and the radio off, tossing ideas around in my head. Nothing clicked. *Come on, come on*, I scolded myself. *Think!*

I'd thought of—and rejected—several possible themes by the time I found a parking spot near the *Girlz* office. I forced a smile on my face as I walked to the door. Mary-Kate was watching for me, and as soon as I stepped inside, she waved at me, grinning broadly.

"Look at what we've been doing," she said. She handed me a printout of the article. "Your pictures turned out great! Don't you just love all the people with their dogs?"

She was right. The article was going to be great. Seeing them all laid out like this, I was proud of the photos I'd taken. There was Dan, the cute guy with the poodle. There was the woman whose hair was the exact same color as her Pomeranian. There was the girl who'd lent Mary-Kate her sweater kissing her schnauzer on the nose.

Hmmm. I studied the photos more carefully. In the photos the resemblance between the people and their dogs was really striking. This was one group of well-groomed pets and owners.

OH. MY. GOSH!

I looked at Mary-Kate for a second, stunned by the major brainstorm that hit me.

"Come on!" I grabbed her by the arm.

"Where are we going?" she yelled as we ran to the car.

"No time to explain. But we've got to get to the park right now. Before it's too late."

chapter eleven

"Are you ready yet?"

Jennifer Lewis poked her head into the back of the display window, looking nervous.

What's she got to be nervous about? I wondered. I'm *the one that needs to be nervous*.

I stood up and groaned, stretching to work out the kinks in my back and legs. Who knew designing a window display was so physical? I'd spent the whole morning climbing a ladder, kneeling on the floor, nailing and stapling, hauling and arranging.

"Are you ready?" Ms. Lewis asked again.

"Not quite," I answered. I turned away from her so that she couldn't see the panic on my face. Time was almost up and my models weren't here yet.

I tacked a corner of fabric down with a hammer. "Almost."

"We need to get started very soon, Ashley," Ms. Lewis warned. She ducked back out.

I sank onto a low rung of the ladder and wiped the sweat off my forehead. I checked my watch again.

They'd promised they'd be here. They sounded so enthusiastic. If they don't show up, my whole idea will be ruined.

I stood up and paced the small space.

Why aren't they here?

I cleared all of my tools and odds and ends into a bin so that the window would be ready when the models arrived. *If* they arrive, I thought to myself.

Ms. Lewis popped her head back in. "We absolutely *must* get started," she said firmly. "I can't keep postponing."

"I know," I said, fighting back tears. I followed Ms. Lewis out of the window, through the store, and into the mall. A crowd had gathered—judges, other store owners, and shoppers. Canvas tarps covered the two display windows so no one would be able to watch Melanie and me hard at work. The windows were about to be revealed—and any minute now, I would be revealed as a total loser.

All my friends were outside the storefront, gathered for the big moment when the winner would be announced. I noticed Melanie standing in front of her covered window, consulting note cards.

I spotted Aaron's face in the crowd. When he smiled at me, I had to force myself to not run and hide. *How can I face them*? I wanted to throw up or cry, but I couldn't do either. Not here. I had to just get through the humiliation somehow.

I'd failed. Melanie would win the contest hands down! And winning might make her become even more of a fashionator—and lose all her friends in the process. And I will have let everyone down.

I had to let Ms. Lewis know that my window was empty, so that she wouldn't be embarrassed too.

I scanned the crowd until I found Ms. Lewis. She had stepped up to the microphone at the podium and was conferring with the judges who stood behind the podium. As I hurried toward her, a security guard motioned me over to him.

"Your guests are here," he told me. "They've been stuck in the freight elevator all this time—but we've finally gotten them out. They're inside the store, waiting for you."

I threw my fist up in the air. "Yes!" I cheered. "I knew they wouldn't let me down."

The security guard smiled and came with me as I made my way through the crowd to Ms. Lewis and the judges.

"Please," I begged, "just five more minutes. We've had an unforeseen circumstance, but it's all fixed now."

"It wasn't the young lady's fault," the security guard said, backing me up.

"I promise I'll be ready to go if I can take just five more minutes. Please."

The judges looked at one another, then finally nodded to Ms. Lewis.

I breathed a huge sigh of relief. "Thank you!" I told the judges. "And thank *you*!" I said to the security guard. I turned and scrambled back through the crowd and back inside the store.

A few frantic minutes later I stood in front of my finished window, still covered with the canvas tarp. I smiled at the crowd. They all looked back at me, confused expressions on their faces.

What's up with them? I wondered. I checked my outfit—no, I didn't have any paint spills or masking tape attached to me anywhere. So why were they all staring?

Then I realized there were all kinds of sounds coming from my window. Because it was covered with the tarp, no one could figure out what was going on inside. It sounded like total chaos—things crashing and bumping. Yelping.

I just smiled and smiled, pretending there was absolutely nothing to be concerned about. I ignored all the commotion behind me and hoped no serious damage was being done.

"Could I have your attention," Ms. Lewis said into the microphone at the podium. "Hello?" She waved her arms to get everyone's attention. "We are ready to begin. It is time to unveil the final entries in the spring break Teen Trend-Spotter Contest!"

Ms. Lewis gestured for Melanie to step up to the microphone. Two stock boys behind her fiddled with some ropes, and the canvas tarp covering Melanie's window dropped to the floor in a heap.

A murmur went through the crowd, and then everyone applauded. Melanie's window was breathtaking.

"'Global Synergy,'" she announced. She held up a hand toward her colorful window. The backdrop alone was gorgeous—it was a detailed map of the world drawn in jewel-toned inks filled in with pale watercolor washes. "What you see here are European, American, South American, Asian, and African fashion accessories. And I bet you can't tell which item is from which country."

She grinned at the crowd as everyone peered at the jewelry, hair clips, purses, boots, scarves, day planners, and all kinds of other accessories draped around cool shelving and small furniture pieces.

"We're all in this together," Melanie said, her voice full of excitement. "I believe fashion is moving toward a celebration of shared cultures and dreams, moving away from an outdated emphasis on differences.

"In ever-increasing ways, we citizens of the world are coming to recognize that together we are all much more than just the sum of our parts."

Wow, I thought as I joined in the applause. Melanie had done an amazing job with her window. I glanced at the judges. They clearly thought so, too.

But Melanie was not quite finished. When the applause died down, she gazed at the crowd, then, I realized, looked straight at me. "In all of our struggles, reaching out to each other is going to be the wave of the future. I hope we can all truly get along and be friends, no matter what."

Melanie stepped back and lowered her eyes. But I had gotten her message. A lump rose in my throat—but in a good way this time.

I didn't have any time to think about Melanie. Ms. Lewis motioned for me to come up to the podium. As I did, the two young men had moved to my window now, and Ms. Lewis signaled to them to drop the tarp. The judges seemed to brace themselves a little, not sure what to expect. I held my breath—not sure what to expect either!

The tarp dropped.

Everybody gasped.

Then laughed.

There in the window were all the adorable dogs and dog owners from the park. Everybody, pets included, wore some type of hat and sunglasses. The dogs and people were all identically trimmed, curled, blow-dried, fluffed, and spiffed, the owners perfectly matched with their pets. Some of them even wore identical outfits.

The effect was totally hilarious.

A banner across the window spelled out my theme: CLEAN-CUT CUTE. Underneath was a subtitle: GROOMING: IT'S NOT JUST FOR DOGS ANYMORE. The back wall held metal shelves filled with sleekly packaged toiletries.

"Greasy hair and stubby chins are a great look for a lot of people," I said, "but with so many new cool products around that make grooming feel like fun, I predict that clean-cut cute is about to make a big comeback."

The huge round of applause almost drowned out the sound of the dogs barking in the window.

I waved my arms like Ms. Lewis had, signaling for quiet so I could continue. "As we all know," I explained as the crowd finally settled down, "dogs are a man's best friend." I grinned. "Woman's, too! The great thing about having a dog for a best friend is you can decide how your dog ought to wear his hair, his collar, even his shades. Human friends like to make their own decisions. That can get frustrating sometimes."

My eyes settled on Melanie's face. I couldn't read her expression at all, but I continued anyway.

"On the other hand, you get a lot of things from a human friend that you can't get from a dog. Like conversation, jokes, encouragement, and . . . even the occasional fashion tip or other friendly advice. And that's why you love them."

Now Melanie smiled. My heart soared—for just a second.

Then I remembered we were still competing with each other.

Would Melanie still smile if I was the one who won? And if she was the winner, would she still give unwanted advice and hurt our friends' feelings?

The biggest question was: Would we still be able to be friends, no matter what happened?

chapter twelve

The crowd outside Glitter and Glam hung around after the unveiling, waiting for the judges' decision. I stood nervously with Aaron, Lauren, and Brittany, chewing my lip. The wait was excruciating.

"You're shaking," Aaron whispered in my ear.

"Nerves, I guess," I said, holding out my trembling hand. I laughed. "Or maybe relief that the contest is over."

"Where should we go to celebrate?" Lauren asked. "No matter what happens, all this hard work deserves a reward!"

Everyone started tossing out suggestions. But my attention was elsewhere—Melanie was making her way through the crowd toward us.

"Hi," she said shyly, pulling a sharply dressed man forward. "Ashley, I'd like you to meet my dad."

Mr. Han smiled warmly. "It is a great pleasure to meet you, Ashley," he said. He had a tiny hint of an accent. "You should be very proud of your accomplishment," he said, shaking my hand. "Congratulations on producing such an inventive and intriguing display."

"Thank you, Mr. Han," I said. He was so sweet, I liked him immediately. "Melanie's window is wonderful, too. You must be very proud of her."

Mr. Han nodded. "I'm always proud of my daughter." He smiled down at Melanie, who blushed. "And now I'd like to go over and inspect those beautiful dogs more closely."

Melanie and I stood side by side, watching him make his way to my window. I really wanted us to be friends again, but I wasn't sure how to begin.

"I'm sorry about the things I said," Melanie said as if she could read my mind. "I'd really like us to be friends again." She held up one hand and put the other on her heart, as if she were making a pledge. "I promise I'll never tell anybody what to wear or how they should fix their hair again ever." She grinned. "I'll save all my fashion advice for my dog."

"You don't have a dog," I said, confused.

"After he saw your window, my dad is suddenly determined to get me a dog," Melanie explained with a big smile. "Just as soon as he figures out which breed is the trendiest."

She giggled. "You know, my dad almost drove me crazy trying to help me with this window. I finally told him I didn't want any advice. I think that's when I realized . . ." She let the sentence trail off, but I knew what she meant. "Anyway, it kind of hurt his feelings at first. But he got over it."

I nodded, understanding completely.

Melanie smiled broadly as she said, "By telling him about this project I found out that he really respects me—and my ideas. He even said he didn't care who won, he was just proud that I took my best shot. And I have you to thank for that."

"I'm glad," I told her.

Melanie paused, then looked at me shyly. "I really mean it. I do want to be friends again. Life is too short and friendships are way too important."

I threw my arms around her. "Of course we're friends." I let her go and took a step back from her. "I really don't care who wins this silly contest as long as we get to celebrate together. The whole point is you and me, daring to try something new and doing our best. In that way, I guess, we've both already won."

"You're the best, Ashley." Melanie hugged me again. I was so glad all the bad feelings were behind us. Now I could truly enjoy finding out who was the winner, because I would be just as happy either way.

"If I could have your attention please." Ms. Lewis stood at the mike again. The crowd quieted down quickly. Everyone wanted to know who the winner was. "The judges have come to a decision."

"About time," Aaron muttered.

Melanie and I both turned to shush him.

He shrugged. "Sorry, but I want to know!"

"And the winner is . . ." Ms. Lewis paused for effect.

"Ashley Olsen!"

"I knew it!" Melanie squealed, turning to hug me once again. "Congratulations, Ashley. That 'clean-cut cute' was such a great, totally original idea. And I know you worked really hard on it."

"Ashley!"

I turned around to see who called out my name.

"Liam," I said, surprised to see him outside of the magazine office. It seemed he had been practically living there.

"I want an exclusive, Ashley. If we hurry, we can fit a two-page spread with photos into this edition before it goes to press." He waved his pen in the air. "'Malibu Teen Predicts the Future!'"

chapter thirteen

"What's going on?" I looked up from my desk in my cubicle at the *Girlz* magazine office, wondering what the sudden noise out in the reception area was all about.

"Isn't C.K. due back right about now?" Liam said. He never took his eyes off the computer screen, where he was manipulating a digital photo for the next issue.

"Oh, that's probably it." I nodded. "It sounds like her. She's all about commotion."

Suddenly, there she was, C.K. breezing past our teeny cubicle, pausing just long enough to stick her head in.

"Mary-Kate. My office. Now."

Uh-oh. I gulped.

"She just walked in the door from Europe and she's already on my case?" I said as I stood up and smoothed my blouse. "This cannot be good news."

I followed C.K. down the hall and into her office. She was speaking before she'd even set down her briefcase.

"I've had some bad news, Mary-Kate, that's going to affect you."

Gulp. I swallowed hard.

"These are hard economic times. Everybody's got to cut back. They've slashed our budget to the bone. So now I have to start making tough decisions, even firing some people." She looked directly at me. "So I decided to start by talking with you."

"Me? You're—you're firing me?" I almost stuttered.

"No, not you." She picked up the phone on her desk and barked into it. "The dummies. Get them in here right now. No, not them, the *page* dummies."

She slammed the phone down. "Sometimes I think I'm the only one with a clue."

"I don't understand," I said, trying to ease her back on track.

"I've seen the article and the photos for your 'Cool Jobs' article," she explained. "It proves that you're a go-getter, the one who makes things happen. No, I'm not letting you go."

"Then . . . then what . . ."

"It's Liam. He has to go. I can't keep you both. I wanted to tell you first because you seem to get along well."

What a disaster!

"But you can't do that," I protested.

"I don't have a choice. I know it's going to mean more work for you, but I think you can manage. I feel bad about this, but my hands are tied." C.K. stood up. "It goes with the territory, I guess. I'm the boss."

"But you can't. It's not—"

She was already out of the office, striding toward the little cubicle where Liam was pouring his heart and soul into the magazine.

I couldn't let this happen. I had to stop her.

I ran after her. "Wait, I have to tell you. . . . It wasn't my—"

She motioned me to be quiet but I couldn't let this happen.

"It's all a mistake."

C.K. stepped just inside the door of our little office. "Liam, we need to talk."

Liam looked up from the keyboard. It was now or never. I threw myself in front of C.K., flinging out my arms.

"It wasn't me!" I shouted. "It wasn't my idea! It was all Liam!"

Stunned silence settled over the entire office. It was as if everybody had stopped breathing.

People strewn around outside our cubicle in the main office edged closer to check out the scene: C.K. standing there with her mouth open, me with my arms out yelling at the boss, and Liam frozen completely speechless, staring at both of us.

"You can't let Liam go," I pleaded. "He's the one with the ideas, not me. The article was his idea, and it would have been nothing without him—his suggestions, his editing, his professionalism, his following your orders exactly and sitting here in the office. I had all the fun—and apparently got all the credit, which I don't deserve."

I paused, but only because I was out of breath.

Liam blushed but looked pleased.

There was a long silence, then C.K. finally spoke. "Both of you. My office. Now."

We followed her down the hall. Everyone stepped out of our way, staring at us. We got into her office, where for the first time in history, she shut the door. "All right, people. Help me get this straight."

I didn't give Liam a chance to talk.

"It's just like I said. The article was Liam's idea. I didn't do much at all, just scribbled a few notes that Liam took and ran with. He has huge talent. If one of us is going to stay, it definitely should be Liam."

Liam looked down, almost digging a hole in the floor with his toe, trying to hide his embarrassment at the praise.

"Is that true, Liam?" C.K. asked.

He looked up. "It's not true that Mary-Kate didn't do much—she did great." He gave me a shy smile. "I think she's going overboard about me. But, yes, it's true, the idea was mine, and I did a lot of work on the piece. And I do think I have some talent for this. And it's definitely true that I'd like to stay."

"What about you, Mary-Kate?" C.K. asked me. "Wouldn't you like to stay?"

"Of course I would," I answered. "But you really need Liam here. This is where he belongs. So I support you one hundred percent in keeping him."

C.K. looked hard at us both, as if we were bugs under a microscope. "All right." She sighed. "Then that's the way it will be." She picked up the phone, shooing us with her hand. "Now get out of here, both of you."

We scurried back to our little office. I could tell Liam wanted to say something, but I held up my hand.

"It's for the best, Liam, really. Now, let's not say anything more about it."

"But, Mary-Kate, what are you going to do?" he asked me, worried.

I smiled. "Oh . . . I'll figure something out," I said.

❀

Taking Mary-Kate on my shopping spree at Glitter and Glam was more fun than anything we'd done for a long time. It was great to just hang out and talk, and laugh, and pick things out for each other.

"I can't believe you're going to be a lifeguard," I said to Mary-Kate as we tried on sunglasses.

"I know. Isn't it awesome?"

"It sounds like fun, but wow, won't that be awfully hard? I mean, all that responsibility."

"I'm up for it," Mary-Kate said. "It's going to be great." Her expression suddenly grew concerned. "Are you sorry the trend-spotting contest is over?"

"It was a blast," I said. "But I think I'd rather just enjoy trends in the present—not predict them for the future."

Mary-Kate laughed. "A lot less pressure that way."

I grinned. "Exactly. Why turn shopping into a job when it's already fun as a sport? But I have to say," I added as we allowed a saleswoman to spritz us with cologne, "I loved the daily challenge. Having deadlines, coming up with ideas . . . that kind of thing."

"You were really good at it," Mary-Kate said, sniffing her wrist and wrinkling her nose.

"Thanks." I rummaged in my purse for some candy and realized my cell-phone message light was blinking. I pulled it out and checked the missed calls log.

"Hey," I told Mary-Kate, "there's a message for me from Ava."

"Ava?" Mary-Kate said as we wandered toward the makeup counters. "The wedding planner who organized Jeanine's wedding? Maybe she wants to hire you! Didn't she say she was going to hire someone for the summer?"

"Do you think so?" I asked. "That would be so cool!"

Mary-Kate grinned. "Only one way to find out!"

"It's no challenge to decide what to do about this phone call," I said, laughing as I dialed the number. I knew whatever would happen next would be exciting.

Find out what happens next in

Sweet 16

Book 15:

CALIFORNIA DREAMS

"Here, Mary-Kate, put your things in this." Tanya, the manager of the Malibu Beach Club, handed me a dark-red tote bag with my name embroidered on one side and "Malibu's Best" embroidered on the other.

"All this stuff is for me?" I couldn't believe it. As if working at one of the hottest beach clubs in town wasn't enough, here was Tanya loading me up with totally fabulous free stuff. And I'd only been here for ten minutes! Today was the first day of my summer job.

The tote bag was huge—big enough to hold my very own deep-red plush towels, matching robe, and two deep-red swimsuits.

"I feel more like a spa guest than an employee." I sighed.

Tanya grinned. "You won't once you start working. It's a tough job. But lifeguards are special people and we try to treat them that way. Come on. I'll take you to the employees' locker room."

I picked up my fabulous red tote bag and followed Tanya out of the office and down a long hallway.

"Here's the locker room," Tanya said. "Get changed and then meet Jon and the other lifeguards by the pool. I'm going to see the catering manager now. Good luck out there."

I ducked into the locker room to change. I couldn't wait to get started!

There was another girl in the locker room. She gave me a friendly smile. "Hi!" she said. "Are you new?"

"Yes. I'm Mary-Kate Olsen."

"I'm Kelly Mason. I worked here last year. It's a great gig."

We chatted while we changed and I could tell we were going to get along great. Five minutes later I was ready. Kelly still had a couple of things to do so I said I'd wait for her in the hall.

I went back out into the hallway all decked out in my new Malibu Beach Club bathing suit, flip-flops, and visor. I caught a glimpse of myself in a mirror that hung on the wall. I looked ready for action!

"Excuse me!" said a deep voice behind me.

I jumped and whirled around. My mouth fell open as I looked up at the totally cute guy who stood there. He was much taller than I was and had strawberry-blond hair and the bluest eyes I'd ever seen.

"Sorry! I didn't mean to scare you," the guy said, smiling down at me. "Jon just asked me to round up everybody for orientation. See you outside."

Kelly came out the locker room door just as he was walking away. "Wow!" she said. "What a hunk. He must be new. What's his name?"

"I don't know," I said, watching him disappear down the hall. But right then and there, I decided I'd make it my business to find out.

mary-kateandashley
so little time
how to train a boy
Now a major TV s
mary-kateandashley.com
mary-kateandashley
so little time
instant boyfriend
Now a major TV series!
mary-kateandashley.com

PARACHUTE PRESS

DUALSTAR PUBLICATIONS

mary-kateandashley.com
AOL Keyword: mary-kateandashley